THE MUTE
BUTTON

Linda S Amstutz

Disclaimer

This is a work of fiction. Names, characters, places, and incidents are the products of the author's warped imagination or are used fictitiously. Any resemblance to actual events, locations, pets, food, or people (living, deceased, or divorced), is purely coincidental.

Original cover artwork and book jacket design by local tattoo artist, Adam Smith

Dedication

This book is dedicated to Ensley, Rebecca, Natalie, and Kathryn. We tried to leave you a safer world with equal playing fields and a belief that all things are possible. I pray you encounter no limits as you continue your journeys with strong minds, brave hearts, and an abundance joy. I love you!

CHAPTER 1

S usan greets every day the same, a fresh Diet Coke and 30 minutes of the *Today Show*. Forty years old and still miraculously carrying the same 125 pounds as the day she graduated from college, Susan pops out of bed and tiptoes to the kitchen to grab a soda can, then crawls back into bed and reaches for the remote. She switches on the television for assurance that all is right with the world, or if not all right, then at least today will not be the day the world comes to an end. Susan begins each day exactly this way, and today is no different.

It's true that she enjoyed the *Today Show* more when Matt Lauer sat at the desk, but she's willing to go Matt-less if it protects the female staff at NBC. Susan admires the work of the #MeToo movement and supports each and every survivor; even if that means that the *Today Show* is a little less interesting. It's a small sacrifice to make for the cause, Susan justifies.

As Susan watches, Al Roker points at the big map of the United States, and she wonders what corny joke he will make about the approaching low front. She has to imagine the joke because the television seems to be muted. Not being in too much of a hurry to hear yet another Al joke, Susan takes her time pushing the Mute button.

Still no sound.

She pushes the Mute button on and off and watches the Mute warning flick on and off across the bottom on the screen. Either way, muted or not muted, Al is silent.

Hmmm. Must be some station problem, Susan decides. Or maybe a Spectrum issue. Or maybe our cable cord needs to be tightened, Susan thinks, counting down all the reasons the audio might not play. And then, while Susan debates rebooting the television, she hears Savannah tell Hoda about some new dessert she tried. And Hoda replies that she thinks the chocolate cherry soufflé sounds heavenly. Smiling, Susan relaxes back on the pillows, confident the sound issue has been resolved.

Then Al sits down next to the ladies and apparently says something. Susan hears Savannah laugh. Susan hears Hoda laugh. Heck, Susan even hears a few of the crew members chortling. Susan hears everyone but Al.

She sits upright. Why can't she hear Al?

Not knowing what to think, Susan instinctively changes channels, just in time to see *The Jerry Springer Show* returning from a commercial break. Susan sits up and listens. Jerry looks into the camera and introduces the next guest, but Susan cannot hear him. Susan only hears the screams of the female audience members. Noting that there are most certainly men in the audience, Susan discovers that she's only hearing the female chanting, "Cheater, cheater, cheater!" A female guest, dressed in a black tube top, leopard leggings and skyscraper heels screams at Susan, "I know he was a cheatin' on me, but I didn't know he was a fatherin' kids, too!"

Usually, this kind of behavior would cause Susan to shake her head in disbelief, but today she leans in closer to the TV, mesmerized, hanging on every word the woman screams.

"You crazy-ass cheater," the woman screams at her boyfriend.

He looks at her and mouths something which seems to infuriate her.

"How dare you say those things to me!" she screams as she picks up her chair and rushes towards him.

Her boyfriend raises his hands, palms outward, towards her and mouths some words, which makes the woman burst into tears. Simultaneously, Susan's eyes fill with tears. Not in any kind of Cheated On Sisterhood way, but with fear.

The camera swivels to Jerry and he talks on and on, occasionally smiling, sometimes shaking his head. Susan quickly turns on the

Close Captioning and begins to read what Jerry is supposedly saying.

"Ladies and gentlemen, who are we to judge? She says she forgives him, he seems repentant. Should we bring out the third corner of this lovers' triangle?"

Susan hears the women in the audience chanting, "Bring her out, bring her out, bring her out!"

Susan quickly changes the channel, surfing through five more morning shows, all with talkative women and silent men. She lands on QVC, where David Venable silently hawks Omaha Steaks. It's so weird to watch him biting into a burger without hearing his MMMMMMmmmmm. Susan pushes the power button on the remote and rolls over.

Sam, oblivious to everything happening, sleeps on his right side, turned away from Susan. She watches his back rise and fall with every deep sleep breath. Tentatively, more nervous in bed than she's been for the past 20 years, Susan reaches over and gently rubs her husband's shoulder.

He stretches and rolls over to face her. As he does every morning, he smiles at Susan before he even opens his eyes.

"Good morning," Susan says quietly.

Sam mouths Good Morning to You.

"What?" Susan asks.

Sam again mouths, Good Morning to You.

"Sam?"

He raises his eyebrows and silently asks Yes?

"Sam, can you hear me?"

He smiles that dazzling smile, the one that stole her heart more than twenty years ago and continues to steal it every single day of her life. He mouths something to her and appears to chuckle. She cannot hear his laugh and that's her favorite sound in the entire world.

Susan starts to cry. "Sam, I cannot hear a word you're saying!!"

Sam looks at her, confused, but she can tell by the look in his eye that he can tell by the look in her eye that she is not only serious, but teetering on a little hysteria. Sam reaches for her and pulls her close to him. He rubs her back and she can feel his head move as he apparently says something to calm her.

And after 20 years of hanging on almost his every word, Susan can no longer hear a single word Sam says.

What the heck is happening here??

CHAPTER 2

F our hours later, Susan's cellphone plays Stevie Wonder's "Isn't She Beautiful" which tells Susan that Lauren is calling.

"Mom? Are you okay?"

"Yes, honey, I'm fine," Susan tries to sound calm. She doesn't want to alarm Lauren who, at age 19, is the Queen of Alarms. She's been hyper-dramatic since the day she was born, when she waited so long to take her first breath that everyone in the Delivery Room was holding theirs. Lauren, the brightest family member, learned to walk at nine months, learned to read at 3 years, and learned to grab center stage at birth. With her golden looks and her chocolate brown eyes, her long arms and gangly legs, her dazzling smile and infectious laugh, it's easy to overlook her hypochondria and over-dramatic reactions to every situation. To Lauren, everything is either catastrophic or the most delirious delight. There is no calm grey area when it comes to Lauren and Susan sure doesn't want her daughter freaking out at college, so when Lauren asks if she's okay, Susan's go-to reply is "I'm fine."

Even today.

Especially today.

"Dad called and told me you can't hear him when he talks. Is he kidding?"

"No, honey, that's true. At least right now. Maybe it's just a temporary thing," Susan says, trying to sound confident.

"Are you playing some kind of joke on Dad?"

"No, honey, I'm not. I just can't hear him right now."

"Seriously, if you're playing a joke, you can tell me. I won't tell. I promise."

"No, I'm not playing a joke. Not about this."

"But you can hear ME........" Lauren says in a higher pitched voice.

"Yes, honey, I'll always hear you. You're my Baby Girl."

"Mom! Not now. This is serious! Something could be very wrong. Dad said you went to see Dr Lee?"

"Yes, honey, Dad insisted I see the doctor."

"What did he say?"

Susan laughs. She just can't help herself. It's really ridiculous, this situation.

"What's so damn funny, Mom?" Lauren asks, her tone changing from concern to irritation.

"Well, honey, I'll tell you; I couldn't hear a word Dr Lee said. Get it? You asked 'What did he say?' And my answer is, 'I don't know. I couldn't hear him,'" Susan laughs again, hoping maybe Lauren will see a little humor here, too.

She doesn't. Instead, she plays the Silent Card. The card that usually precedes the Pout Card. Susan waits, hoping that Lauren won't throw a hissy fit, not today.   Somehow Lauren always manages to make everything about HER and while Susan usually watches this transformation with amusement and, to be honest, a little bit of awe, Susan just doesn't have the patience to play this game today. Instead, she caves and drives the conversation forward by explaining, "Dr Lee and Dad talked and talked and talked and finally they brought in a nurse who acted like a translator, telling me what they said."

"That must have felt weird," Lauren empathizes with her mom.

"You're right, it did. And here's the weirdest part, Dr Lee would talk and talk to Dad and me and then the nurse would just tell me a short translation. And they all laughed a lot. I think they thought this was a joke or something."

"It's not a joke, Mom, though is it? Mom?" Lauren almost pleads.

"No, honey, it's not a joke. I swear. Although I can kinda see the humor of the situation."

"Mom, I did a little research before I called you. You know, my roommate Maya is pre-med, and so we went online and did a little research. She thought maybe you had a form of aphasia, so we Googled it. Do you know what that is?"

"Google? Of course! Everyone knows Google. Even moms," Susan laughs again, thinking maybe she is doing a little too much laughing. But this whole thing is so ridiculous.

"No, Mom! I know you know Google. But do you know what Aphasia is?"

"Oh, Yes! It's the inability to process words. Like after you have a stroke. Did you learn anything helpful?"

"According to our sources," Lauren continues, in an authoritative voice, "There are several forms of aphasia. There's Anomic Aphasia, which is the least severe and is simply when the correct word is known to the patient but you can't say it. Like it's on the tip of your tongue. That doesn't apply to you."

"Nope, I don't have anything on the tip of my tongue," Susan smiles.

"Look, Mom, this is serious. Take this seriously," Lauren warns, now sounding like she's the adult and Susan is the child. "There's also Broca's Aphasia where you cannot accurately produce a correct word or finish a complete sentence. There's Wernicke's Aphasia where you are unaware that you are producing nonsensical words. There's Global Aphasia, that's like Grandma had, where you lose all function of spoken word and even have trouble understanding."

"So all the aphasias have more to do with trouble speaking, not hearing, is that right?"

"That's right, Mom. What did Dr Lee say? Seriously. Tell me."

"He couldn't find anything wrong, honey. He's sending me to a neurologist for some tests but he doesn't think they will find anything."

"He doesn't? How in the world can that be? Doesn't he believe you that something is terribly, terribly wrong here?" Susan hears the panic growing behind Lauren's words.

"Honey, he does believe that I believe. Ha! He wants me to see a psychologist."

"Does Dad agree?"

"Oh, your dad has always wanted me to see a psychologist." Susan laughs again.

"Mom, there's something else I read about.........." Lauren says, not joining in her mom's laughter.

"Yes, honey?"

"There's this thing called Selective Deafness......." Lauren lets her voice trail off dramatically.

"What's that?" Susan asks.

"It's when a person can filter out a specific noise or sound and become deaf to it."

"What do you mean?" Susan listens a little more closely. Maybe Lauren's onto something.

"Like when I'm cramming for an exam and I'm listening to music and then I start concentrating so hard on my study material that I no longer even hear my music. That's Selective Deafness."

"I see."

"Here's another example: you know how if you're staying in a hotel for a couple of nights and the first night there, you can't sleep because every time someone walks down the hall between the rooms, or shuts a door too loudly in the room next to you, it keeps you awake and you can't sleep a wink? You know what I mean? But then, after a night or two, you get used to those sounds and you sleep like a baby all night long, no matter how many people walk up and down the halls? Because you have Selective Deafness for those hall noises. Get it?"

"I get it. I understand. And yes, I guess we all have had Selective Deafness from time to time. But, are you saying you think I am purposely not hearing Dad? Or any man?"

"Mom, do you remember that joke your friend Cindy used to tell? 'My husband has a mute button in his brain that is activated by the sound of my voice'?"

"Ohhhhhhhhhhhh," Susan doesn't really know what else to say, so she stalls with the longest ohhhhhhhhh she can muster.

"Mom, do you think that you have a mute button that is activated by the sound of a man's voice?"

And Susan has no answer for this because the very thought is so foreign to her. It hasn't crossed her mind, until just now, when

Lauren says the words. And then Susan questions herself. Can I just be muting out men's voices?

Can it be that simple?

And why would I do such a thing?

Am I that angry?

Or resentful?

Or impatient?

Do I hate men that much?

CHAPTER 3

When Susan's phone pings that she's receiving a text message at 11 pm, she knows, without looking, who is messaging her.

LAUREN: *My calc profs voice is growing faintr. Cd hrdly hear hs lecture 2day. Is ths how ur deafness bgan?*

SUSAN: *No, Lauren. Mine happened all at once.*

LAUREN: *Do U think it's hereditary?*

SUSAN: *No, I don't.*

LAUREN: *Do U think it's contagious?*

SUSAN: *No, honey, I don't.*

LAUREN: *Do U think it cn happen 2 me?*

SUSAN: *No, honey, not a chance.*

LAUREN: *Mom, R U scared?*

SUSAN: *I'm not scared. And you shouldn't be, either. I'm more curious as to how long this will last and what I can do about it..........*

LAUREN: *What if it doesn't go away?*

SUSAN: *IDK. It's too early to worry about that. And it's too late at night to think such sad thoughts.*

LAUREN: *What about Dad? U can't even hear him.*

SUSAN: *Dad has been texting me. Congratulations, I
            finally got him texting. LOL. Seriously, I
            really do miss the sound of his voice.*

SUSAN: *We'll be ok, Lauren. Dad and I will be ok, no
            matter what, and you will be, too.*

LAUREN: *I hope so. I really do.*

LAUREN: *Mom?*

SUSAN: *Yes, honey?*

LAUREN: *Cn U hear music? Like JT's new cd? Can U
            hear him sing?*

SUSAN: *Oh! Male singers! I haven't checked. Let me
            see. BRB.*

After what seems like the longest pause, the texting between
mother and daughter continues..........

SUSAN:  *No Bruno Mars!!!!*

LAUREN: *OH MOM!!!!*

SUSAN: *OMG! I can't even hear the Beatles.*

LAUREN: *IKR*

LAUREN: *Mom?*

SUSAN: *Yes, honey??*

LAUREN: *I love U mom. I'm sorry this is happening 2 U.*

SUSAN: *I love you, too, Lauren. More than words can say.*

LAUREN: *U still having Susan Supper 2morrow?*

SUSAN: *Yes, I'm planning on it. Won't they be surprised at this turn of events?*

LAUREN: *Yes, I'm sure. TTYL?*

SUSAN: *Yes, honey. And don't worry. Everything is going to be okay. Love you lots!!!*

LAUREN: *Me, too. Love U!! Night!!!*

CHAPTER 4

S usan Supper happens the third Wednesday of every
month. Just four friends having dinner out, laughing,
eating, drinking, listening to each other and bearing
witness to each other's lives.

And they just happen to share the same first name.

This is how it started: About ten years ago, Sam and Susan
brought a pan of freshly-baked brownies to their new neighbors.
Sam loves this "Welcome to the 'Hood" tradition so much that he
even bakes the brownies. And delivers them. Usually alone and then
returns to Susan with the scoop on the newest neighbors. This time,
though, it was a warm spring evening and Susan decided to
accompany him. Nothing is prettier than a South Carolina spring
evening, when the sky is just beginning to darken and the dogwood

blossoms seem to glow with the last rays of the setting sun. The azalea blossoms were definitely fighting for attention, but the dogwoods wouldn't give up center stage. So pretty and dainty and yet somehow proud, they always touched Susan's heart. Every spring. So when Sam said he wanted to greet the new neighbors, Susan asked to tag along.

"Of course, come with me. And when we're done visiting, let's take a stroll around the block. Rumor has it there's a full moon tonight and I'd love to steal a kiss from you in the moonlight."

"Steal a kiss? Baby, I'll give you a dozen kisses," Susan puckered up and air-kissed Sam as she grabbed her house keys.

The new neighbors were a delight. Larry, the husband, worked from home as a Digital Forensics Investigator and looked like your stereotypical computer geek, black-framed glasses, pale complexion and all, and was not only an expert at Digital Forensics, but also at puns. Susan Wood, a well-known and respected ceramic artisan who had several successful shows in both Charlotte and Charleston, was his wife. They didn't have any children, but were doting parents to four miniature Dachshunds named Margie, Mandy, Minnie, and Mickey. Their house overflowed with laughter, barking, and the clickety-clacking of doggie nails across hardwood floors.

Susan Wood, christened Susan O'Brien, didn't have any pets growing up. She was raised in a no-nonsense, deeply religious family, where piousness was held as the highest virtue, followed closely by humility. Two of Susan's uncles were priests. One aunt was a nun. And Susan's older brother was a Jesuit priest. Their family had more rosaries than casserole dishes and Susan was expected to follow everyone's example and place her future in the hands of the Almighty Lord. This was reinforced on a regular basis as Susan attended parochial elementary school, catholic high school, and finally, College of Saint Mary.

Susan was a good Catholic girl, she stuck out her tongue every Sunday to receive the Body of Christ and she regularly searched her soul for shortcomings in the confessional booth. As an act of penance for all the sins of the world, Susan never painted her nails, never wore make up, and let her hair grow straight down her back until the day, every 24 months, when she had her hair clipped off for Locks of Love. While Susan never set her eyes at sainthood, she tried to be honest and fair and loving to all of God's creatures.

And then her senior year of college, Susan noticed boys. As with most late-bloomers, when the hormones kicked in, they kicked hard. Suddenly, boys were everywhere.

Tall boys.

Blonde boys.

Brunette boys.

Football players.

Tennis players.

Smart boys.

Dumb boys.

Boys who could make your heart pump hard on a dance floor.

Boys who could make your heart pump hard............

It was right in the midst of all this heart pumping, Susan met Larry Wood. One day, walking through the local nursery, trying to find the perfect African violet pot, Susan looked across the row of pottery and saw him standing there. Not just standing there, but looking at her.

With an African violet pot in his hands.

Susan's heart pumped even harder.

And even though Cosmo magazine (devoured monthly and then tossed in the trash can behind the PoliSci building) strongly advised against it, Susan followed Larry out of the nursery. She followed him to a diner where they shared a strawberry milkshake and a large order of French fries and no one played hard to get. From that day forth, they only had eyes for each other and miraculously, made it three weeks past graduation before they eloped. Susan's father cried at the news, but Susan's mother immediately embraced this new son-in-law and started his conversion into Catholicism.

Larry negotiated his way through several job offers and soon Susan and he moved to Nashville, where Larry worked on some government computer system, while Susan discovered the joy of sticking her hands, wrist deep, into wet clay. Almost like a prayer, every morning, Susan began her day in clay. She made bowls and pots and pitchers and she taught herself how to glaze and fire her creations.

Creations. That's exactly how she thought of her pottery. Each one, crafted by her own bare hands, was a sacrament to her. Made with love and joy, Susan's creations were her second love. She hired a handyman to line the garage with shelves and filled the shelves with pottery. On their first wedding anniversary, Larry bought Susan her own kiln. That Christmas, he bought her a pottery wheel and as much clay as he could carry in the back of his Jeep.

Whenever Susan carried one of her bowls to the weekly neighborhood pot luck dinners, some neighbor invariably begged to buy it from her. Pasta salad and all. It went from there to neighbors knocking on her door, begging to browse through the shelves of pottery for Christmas, birthday, and housewarming gifts. Just as Susan's side business was starting to pick up, Larry received a dream job offer and announced it was time for them to move to Columbia, SC.

Ever the dutiful wife, Susan packed up her ceramics and rosaries and they moved south into the land of pollen, avid football fans, Palmetto bugs, and a scarcity of Catholic churches. Susan didn't resent the move; in fact, she fell in love with the magnolia trees and the hills of azaleas. She even loved the kudzu. This place felt like home. Within months, Susan's pottery was on exhibit in several artsy gift shops and Susan's career was off and running. Oh, and as a show of gratitude for being such a good sport about moving, Larry turned their two-car garage into a first-class art studio for Susan.

In the midst of all this joy and creativity, Susan and Sam knocked on their front door, bringing brownies and friendship.

The two Susans immediately formed a bond over their shared name. "Who were you named after?" "Do you know what the name

Susan means in Hebrew?" "Omigod, have you ever looked at all the Urban Dictionary terms with the name Susan?" "Did you ever hear of a Musty Susan?" They laughed and discovered a shared interest in the arts, Susan Wood's passion falling on ceramics while Susan Strickland illustrated books, specializing in children's books. They discovered not only did they both work in the arts; they both practiced their art from home studios. Although Susan W had been more successful in her trade, and gained more recognition, their ardor for their craftsmanship was equal, and only surpassed by their love of pasta and desserts. They scheduled a dinner date for the following day.

From then on, the two Susans met for dinner at least once a month. And always at locally owned establishments. That was one of their two rules: No Chain Restaurants and no Fast Food Joints. Usually they dined in Columbia, but they didn't hesitate to drive over to Lexington or up to Charlotte if some restaurant was well reviewed. Susan W's favorite meal was Seafood Fettucine Alfredo while Susan S was crazy about any kind of ravioli. They both loved to eat, loved to talk, loved their husbands, and their only real difference of opinions was religion. Susan W still reverently practiced Catholicism while Susan S embraced her belief in reincarnation.

"You should come with me sometime for one of the holiday masses. They are spectacular with choir and trumpets and even incense. It's so moving."

"Maybe I'll try that in my next life," Susan S joked, always one to look for a laugh.

During the fall of that first year of delicious Susan Suppers, they found Susan Meroni. That's back when Susan M was still in her mid 20's, wore her hair in braids, and waitressed at Pasta Fresca.

After listening to the nightly specials, Susan S asked, "Did you say your name was Susan?"

"Yes, it is. Named after my mom's sister..........."

"MY name's Susan," interrupted Susan W.

"Oh yeah? MY name's Susan, too!" added Susan S.

"Are you two making fun of me?" Susan Meroni, soon to be dubbed Susan M, asked.

"Never. We'd never mock another Susan," someone said as all three women started talking at once, comparing notes, exchanging compliments, laughing and doing all the things women do when they connect with a kindred spirit.

Susan M kept coming back to the table, checking on the other two Susans, bringing them extra garlic bread, filling their water glasses and comping them a couple of blackberry mojitos.

"What time does your shift end?" asked Susan W.

"Eight o'clock. Only about 15 minutes left, actually," Susan M checked her Fitbit for the time.

"Do you have to rush right home?" asked Susan S, nodding toward Susan W, who smiled and nodded back.

"Not really. I'd have to call my mom and make sure she can keep the kids a little longer. What do you have in mind?" Susan M asked, eyes twinkling, head tilted, looking like she was ready for anything.

"Why don't you hang out with us for a while? We can share a dessert. You might be a few years younger than us, but I think you're one of our tribe," Susan W touched Susan M's arm.

Susan M's grin spread across her face.

"Oh, she's one of us," Susan S agreed. "I knew it right away!"

"Hahahahaha, you had her at Ravioli!!!!!" Susan W practically shouted, she was laughing so hard.

"Yes! Omigosh, yes! I'll be back shortly. Dessert's on me!" Susan M bounced off, her smile so bright it warmed the room.

They sat there, at Pasta Fresca, until the place closed down. Then they walked to the parking lot and stood there and talked for another hour, baring their souls to each other.

"I have 3 kids, who I love dearly, but hadn't planned on. Every single one was a complete surprise. Guess I'm an easy person to surprise. Or maybe I'm just easy!!" Susan M shared while the other two Susans laughed.

"Are you married?"

"Not any more. Not as of last week. It was the last surprise I got from my husband; I discovered he had impregnated the checkout girl at Whole Foods. I wondered why he kept bringing home so many of those Mock Chicken Salads. I thought he was just really getting interested in healthy eating!"

The three Susans scowled, and then all three shook their heads in unison, like they were backup singers.

"Are you from here, Susan?" asked Susan S.

"Yes, born right here at Richland Memorial. My mom and dad are from here, too. So are my grandparents. I guess my roots run deep in this place."

"And have you always lived here, then?"

"I have. The furthest I've made it from here is Myrtle Beach. Oh wait, I did go to Savannah, Georgia one St Patrick's Day. As a matter of fact, that's how I got my firstborn, Patrick! I tell him I found him under a four leaf clover!!" Susan blushed, then laughed and the other Susans laughed and found Susan adorable.

"His dad's not a leprechaun, is he?" Susan S joked.

"No, he was the grand marshal of the parade. You don't think I'd sleep with just any guy in a green suit, do you?" Susan M laughed at her own joke.

"And do all of your kids have such interesting conception stories?"

"Let me think……. Patrick was conceived under the rainbow, right next to the pot of gold that Saint Patrick's Day," Susan M was actually counting her kids off with her fingers. As she lifted finger Number Two, she exclaimed, "Oprah was conceived in the balcony of the Nickelodeon Theatre between anniversary airings of *The Color Purple*.

Susan S and Susan W almost fell over laughing. "Was her father an usher?" one of them asked, gasping for air.

"Of course not. I wouldn't sleep with an usher. Oprah's daddy was the projectionist."

The three friends just looked at each other, two of them wondering if this was a serious answer and then Susan W and Susan S saw the twinkle spark out of Susan M's eyes and their laughter doubled.

"And your third child?"

"Oh, you mean Barack?"

Susan S and Susan W stood there, mouths wide open, afraid to even make eye contact with each other.

Without blinking an eye, Susan M continued, "Barack was conceived on the night of Barack Obama's inauguration. You remember when Beyonce sang "At Last" at the Inaugural Ball?"

"How could we forget? Most romantic inauguration dance EVER!"

"Right. Very romantic. And I'm a romantic at heart." Susan M nodded and the other two Susans couldn't disagree. "So, I was home alone that night, my mom was having a sleepover with Oprah and Patrick, and I'm watching all the inauguration stuff on tv and I'm just busting with pride over our country and how we just elected our first African American president, and how maybe next time we could maybe elect a woman, or at least in my lifetime we might elect a woman, and I got so sentimental that I called my neighbor over to watch the rest of the inaugural ball with me and then Beyonce starts singing that damn song, and we got up and started dancing with Barack and Michelle and, man, I was feeling all my feels and then, BOOM, we made Barack."

Susan S and Susan W nodded.

"And so you married Barack's daddy?"

"Oh, I married all their daddies. None of them turned out to be keepers, but they all gave me the best kids any mom could ever want. I always wanted to be part of a big happy family, so I made my own. Me, Patrick, Oprah, and Barry. A big happy family."

"How do you manage? I mean, financially," asked Susan S.

"If you don't mind us asking......" interrupted Susan W.

"No, I don't mind. Well, of course, I get a little child support. Not always on time, but they usually come through. And then I work here part-time while my mom keeps the kids, or while they visit with their daddies. And in my spare time, I bake and sell birthday cakes. You know, special ones, like super heroes or cakes shaped like unicorns or football mascots. Whatever."

"Wow, you are busy!" Susan W exclaimed.

"Where do you get the energy?" Susan S asked.

"It's her age," declared Susan W. "She's still sipping from the fountain of youth!"

"Nope. No fountain of youth here. I lick a lot of frosting bowls! Sugar, you know, I practically mainline sugar!"

So that's how Susan S found Susan W and how, together, they found Susan M. They thought their circle was complete, but sometimes in life, just when you think you have everything you need and you know exactly how the story goes, life gives you a surprise. Sometimes it's an unexpected pregnancy, sometimes it's another Susan.

During her junior year of high school, Lauren brought the final Susan into her mother's life. It was the night of her Junior Prom and after Susan and Sam took about a thousand photos of their only daughter in her first prom dress (black lace, can you imagine?), Susan drove Lauren to her date's house. His name was Mike and Susan always believed that Mike was Lauren's First Love. You know First Love, the one you remember the rest of your life, with a smile, if you're one of the lucky ones? Susan and Lauren spent many late nights lying side by side on Lauren's bed, discussing love and possibilities and love and responsibilities and love and compromises and love and how it's possible to love someone with your whole heart and yet love yourself at the same time.

Susan walked Lauren up to the well-lit porch of Mike's parents and was met by Mike's dad, "Hi, I'm Will," he said, offering his hand to Susan and then turning to Lauren and exclaiming, "Who is this beauty? You look like a movie star!!" Lauren giggled. Mike appeared, looking more like a man than a boy in his dark grey suit. He offered his hand to Lauren and held her elbow as she stepped up into the living room, explaining, "I'm sorry, Lauren, but my mom is insisting we pose for some pics."

"That's right, that's so damn right," laughed a short, well-muscled woman wearing spandex running pants and a tight tank top.

"Hi, I'm Susan Abbey, Mike's Mom," she proclaimed, shifting the camera into her left hand, while offering her right hand out first to Lauren, "It's so nice to finally meet you, Mike says the most wonderful things about you..." and then she turned toward Susan S and exclaimed, "Your daughter is lovely. Mike will take excellent care of her tonight, won't you, Mike?"

Mike nodded and blushed.

"Nice to meet you, Susan. Guess what? I'm a Susan, too..." Susan S exclaimed, more delighted than surprised. By this time in her life, Susan S always expected the unexpected. She was not one to turn her nose up to any of life's great gifts, and this Susan Abbey seemed like a big, whopping, jumping-out-of-a-cake kind of gift.

"Well, I'll be damned. We're both named Susan. What's the chance of that?"

A thousand more photos were taken of Lauren and Mike and then Will drove them to Prom while the two Susans chatted.

"I don't know if Mike told you, but we just moved here a year ago. Will was transferred with his job. We love it here, although the job thing isn't working out so well."

"I'm sorry. Glad you like it here, though. We think Mike's a great guy."

"Thanks, I think so, too. They sure looked cute together, didn't they? Do you remember your Junior Prom?"

The Susans reminisced about their own high school and college proms and soon Susan A confided that she and Will were having marital problems.

"We're kind of a couple of convenience, if you know what I mean. Separate bedrooms, common goals, just trying to be kind to each other and get this wonderful kid raised together, ya know?"

"I understand."

"Will's a great guy, don't get me wrong. For me, it's just hard to have to share so much of my life with another person. I don't want to check with someone else if I want to spend my whole day planting hosta bulbs, ya know? Or I hate having to explain when I want to take a run under the stars at 3 am. Ya know what I mean?"

"I get it. Marriage isn't for everyone. And not all marriages are created equal."

"Right. So. You wanna see my garden? Don't worry, it's well lit," Susan A jumped up and led the way through the immaculate house and out to the back yard and into someplace magical. Brick walkways wandered in and out of snowball bushes and camellias while hostas lined the walkways. Susan S was practically speechless.

Practically.

"Look, I have a couple of friends named Susan and we get together once a month for supper out. I think you'd love us. Could you could tear yourself away from all this splendor and have dinner and a few laughs with three kindred spirits?"

"I don't know," Susan A responded, looking down at her shoes and shaking her head. "I've tried to have groups of girlfriends before and it always turns into a drama. Someone gossips too much. Or someone is too snarky. And then there's that whole jealousy thing with women. Someone is always trying to outdo someone else. Whose purse cost more? Whose house is bigger? Who has the smartest kid? That kind of crap. I've sworn off it, ya know?

"I do know," Susan S agreed, "I know exactly what you mean. But here's the thing, our little group is not like that. For some reason, we have this idealistic respect for each other and consider our Susan Suppers to be a sacred no-judgement zone. We honestly support each other and give each other enough room to be ourselves. And you, my new lady friend, would fit right in........."

And even though Susan S was a head taller and ten pounds heavier, Susan A grabbed her by the waist, lifted her, and spun her around right under the magnolia tree.

"Yes, ma'am, I damn well do!!"

And while the romance between Lauren and Mike ended only a week after prom, Susan A and Susan S kept going strong.

And that's how Susan S found Susan W and how, together, they found Susan M, and then Susan A joined them and they were one in heart and soul. Nothing binds women more permanently than pasta and laughter.

So here it is, almost five years later and the four Susans squeeze into a booth at Casa Linda. Someone orders a pitcher of margaritas and an order of queso dip and chips. They exchange compliments,

"Did you lose weight?" being the most popular, closely followed by "I love your necklace. Is that new?"

As soon as the drinks are poured into the chilled glasses, Susan S starts talking, "So. I've got some weird news."

"Weird for you or just plain weird?" Susan A jokes and the others laugh. They know exactly what she means. Susan S is known for getting some pretty quirky, weird ideas sometimes.

"Weird. Just really weird. And a little scary," Susan S explains, stopping to sip her drink. She looks at the faces of her friends to make sure they are listening, and then she leans closer to them and continues in a quieter voice, "I woke up the other morning with some kind of hearing problem."

"What do you mean?" asked Susan W, reaching out to touch her friend's arm. "Are you ill?"

"No, I don't think so. Everything else seems just fine. Just this one hearing thing."

"So what? You can't hear everything? Can you hear me?" Susan M asks loudly.

"Yes, I can hear you just fine. I can hear all of you just fine," Susan S sips her margarita and then just blurts out, "I cannot hear any man's voice."

The other three Susans sit and look at each other for about thirty seconds and then, simultaneously, burst into loud laughter. Susan M, who's never had any kind of good luck with men, raises her margarita glass and says, "Lucky you!!! Here's to no more ManSplaining!"

"And no more 'Have you seen my car keys?'"

They laugh again and even though Susan S knows this is a serious situation, she still sees the humor in it and she joins in their laughter. As a matter of fact, she laughs the hardest. She laughs and laughs until her eyes fill with tears.

"Seriously, though. What's the damn story?" asks Susan A.

"I really don't know. I just can't hear any man speak."

"Not any man? What about Sam? Can you hear him?" asks Susan W.

"Nope."

The Susans nod and think about this. Susan A tries to relieve the tension with a joke, "I wish I hadn't been able to hear Will all those years."

"I hear that," agrees Susan M. "My life would be easier with no men's voices. Hey, what about men on tv? Can you hear them?"

"Nope."

"Not even Red Reddington?"

"Not even Red."

"How about the males in movies?" asks Susan M, full of questions.

"Not one word."

The laughter stops then while the Susans think about this.

Susan M, needing more clarification, asks, "Can you hear male voices on the radio? Can you hear Barry Manilow music?"

"I can hear the music, but not his singing."

"Holy shit!" shouts Susan A, then covers her mouth and looks around to make sure she hasn't created yet another scene. "Can you not hear ANY male voices?"

"Well, it seems I can hear the voices of little boys. See those little boys over there?" Susan S nods to the long table that overflows with happy parents and a gaggle of young kids, all pushing and playing and one of the boys declaring, "Mom, he spit in my drink!"

"I heard that! I can hear those little boys."

"But not their dads?" asks Susan W.

"That's right."

"How damn interesting........" says Susan M. "I wonder if your breaking point is puberty? And if it is, I wonder what that means......"

"This is too damn weird," shouts Susan A, as she reaches for her margarita and shakes her head.

"What's your doctor say?" asks calm Susan W.

"They can't find anything wrong. They say it's probably some emotional response to something." Susan S finishes her margarita and refills her glass.

And then the Susans do something they have never done before, they grow silent. Each one lost in her own thoughts. A minute or two later, the waiter appears and everyone places her order. Susan S knows it's her turn when the waiter looks at her. The other Susans watch as the waiter asks her if she'd like black or pinto beans with her dinner and Susan S doesn't answer. Susan W prompts her, "You'd like the black beans, wouldn't you?"

As the waiter walks away, Susan A says, "Damn! You really couldn't hear him, could you?"

Susan S shakes her head no.

Again the Susans think about this. Susan M breaks the silence, "Boy, if I couldn't hear any man's voice, the one I'd really miss would be Anderson Cooper. Can you imagine a life without hearing the voice of Anderson Cooper? That giggle, I mean, c'mon …."

The other Susans nod and Susan W chimes in, "I can't imagine a world without Morgan Freeman's voice!"

"Yes," they chime in together.

"Imagine *Shawshank Redemption* without Morgan Freeman's voice. And what about not hearing Christopher Walken's voice?" asks Susan A. "Now that would be a damn pity."

"Or that guy who plays Negan. He's got a voice that makes me wet," Susan M adds.

"Every man's voice makes you wet," Susan A twinkles her eyes at Susan M. Susan A sticks her tongue out at Susan M and responds, "I bet you wish you could get wet!"

They all laugh because Susan A has recently declared herself celibate.

The laughter is broken by Susan S declaring, "Besides Sam, of course, the voice I most long to hear right now is Mr Rogers. I really need to hear him tell me that everything's going to be okay."

They let that sink in for a minute, and then Susan A suggests, "Let's drink to that!"

Their dinners arrive and as they eat, Susan W asks, "Susan, did anything traumatic happen before you lost your hearing?"

"Not really. Sam and I did have an argument the night before. And we went to bed mad at each other. But all couples do that sometimes, right?"

"Don't ask me," Susan A says. "Those days are over for me. Since the divorce, I sleep like a baby – right in the middle of the damn bed, too!"

"Yes, we all argue with our spouses from time to time," Susan W responds. "Even Larry, if you can you imagine, gets peckish from time to time."

"Well, I don't have any of that to worry about," Susan M chimes in, "Now that I'm baking full time, the only thing that talks back to me is fondant."

"How's that going? Has business been good?"

"Yes, business is great. And every time a new Disney movie comes out, I'm swamped with orders for character cakes. It's a lot of work, but I love it. I'm even thinking about hiring an assistant. Someone to bake and leave me with more time to decorate. And I'm grateful that y'all nudged me into taking the big step."

"Nudged? I think we out and out pushed your damn ass out of the waitress apron and into a baker's hair net!"

"Those cupcakes you made for my pottery show were works of art! Everyone was in love with them," Susan W says.

"Speaking of your pottery show, I read the review in Free Times. Way to go, girl!"

"I was lucky everyone was so into those bowls. I wasn't sure if they'd be well received or not."

"Oh, I love those damn bowls! I put my three in a row on the center of my dining room table. Who, but you, would think to paint inspirational words on beautiful bowls? And the red She Persisted bowls sold out almost as soon as you opened the doors. I hope you'll make more of those."

"How can I not, with the current administration?"

"I wish you'd make a damned bowl that screamed Impeachment. And then glaze it in a peach color. Oh!! Or just a bowl that said IM and is shaped like a peach!"

The Susans laugh, and Susan W makes a note on her phone. When she finishes, she looks up and asks, "So, how is the landscaping business, Susan?" They all turn and look at Susan A.

"A little slow. It's so seasonal, ya know? Busy as an aphid one month, slow as a damn slug the next," Susan A explains. "Did I tell you I'm building a greenhouse on the lot? Can't wait to start germinating seeds."

"Speaking of germinating…….." Susan M says, with a twinkle in her eye, and a pat to her tummy.

"Noooooooooo waaaaaaaay," the other three Susans exclaim, not in disapproval, but more in astonishment and delight.

"Are you really pregnant?" Susan W asks.

"Yes, ma'am. Just confirmed it this morning. Another bun in the oven," Susan laughs. "I'm never happier than when I'm pregnant. Let's hope Dave doesn't mind."

"You haven't told him yet?" asks Susan S.

"No, I wanted my Susans to be the first to know. Who wants to be a Godmother?"

"Me, me, me, it's my damn turn!" shouts Susan A. "I can't wait to hold another baby. No one makes sweeter babies than you. Do you have a name picked out?"

"Maybe. You'll have to wait and see. And now, let me push away this margarita glass and quit pretending to drink from it."

Susan A grabs the glass, holds it in the air, and says, "Here's to Susan and her baby!"

"I love when everyone is in such a good place," starts Susan W. "I know you have this male deafness thing happening, Susan, but I feel like it's going to clear itself right up."

"Yeah, and I can think of a lot worse things than not hearing a man speak!" Susan A laughs.

"But wait a minute," Susan W interrupts, "Don't you have to teach that class at Midland Tech pretty soon?"

Susan S nods her head.

"How will you teach a class if you can't hear the male students when they speak?" asks Susan M.

"Yeah, that's going to be damn tricky," adds Susan A.

"I still have a couple of months until then. I'm hoping that I'll be hearing by then," Susan S says, nervously.

"And when is your appointment with the therapist?"

"It's on Friday morning. It can't get here soon enough."

CHAPTER 5

Bella Washington's office sits above a busy bookstore on Devine Street. The two businesses, both therapeutic in their own ways, share the same glass outer door, but have separate doorways inside the atrium. Booklovers enter the world of written words to the right; Bella's clients climb a flight of stairs to enter her world of spoken words and shared secrets.

Bella herself looks about 60 years old and has been practicing psychotherapy most of her adult life. She seems to have seen everything and is virtually unshakable, either that or she has mastered the best poker face this side of Las Vegas. Her very posture exudes a quiet, calm that soothes even the most manic patient. Her voice, high and sweet, can coax even the deepest buried secrets to show themselves. Years ago, when Lauren was first entering her teen years, it was Bella who helped Susan find a way to parent and not lose her mind, or daughter, in the process. Susan worked hard and was proud to say she was the first mother in three generations of her family who wasn't estranged from her daughter. So far, so good. Susan always attributes this success to Bella's coaching so when this whole selective deafness thing happened, Susan was confident it was Bella who would rescue her.

"It was so nice of you to see me on such short notice. It's been years since I was last here. Do you remember?" Susan asks, as she plops down on the white leather chair, saving the couch for another day.

Bella sits across from her, in a matching chair. "Yes, Susan, I remember you. I enjoyed our sessions and still have my file on you. How's Lauren these days?"

"Oh, she's great. Getting ready to finish college soon."

"I'm happy to hear that. And Sam, how's he?"

"Sam's good. Being a good sport about his wife not hearing a word he says." Susan sighs and shakes her head.

"How is that going? How do you communicate?" Bella grabs her notebook and scribbles as she's talking with Susan.

"Well, I talk to him, just as I've always. And he responds with body language or with texting. He texts me most things. At first he texted a lot, but the longer this goes on, his texting happens less frequently. And sometimes he just sends me an emoticon." Susan frowns. "I think I might be trying his patience."

"Well, you're not doing it on purpose."

"No, I know. He knows. Still, I'd feel the same way if he couldn't hear me."

"Would you?"

"Hmmmm. Would I? Good question, really. I mean, sometimes it feels like he never hears me anyway, even though he isn't having any hearing issues. Hmmmmm."

"Susan, right before you lost your hearing, did anything unusual happen?" Bella looks into Susan's eyes and watches her closely.

"Not really. Not that I can think of. I mean, Sam and I had an argument the night before, but nothing more than the usual kind of argument. Like most married couples," Susan looks at Bella to see if Bella is nodding in agreement. Bella doesn't nod, but smiles at Susan.

"What was the argument about?"

"It's stupid. Like most arguments, I guess. He thinks we should join his side of the family on our summer vacation, rent a house with them all at some mountain resort or something. I think we should take Lauren and go off somewhere, just the three of us, before she's all grown up and we don't have her to ourselves anymore."

"I see. And what was the conclusion of the discussion?"

"There wasn't really a conclusion. He said we should sleep on it and discuss it later, and I said he wasn't really acknowledging my feelings. We ended up rolling away from each other and going to sleep mad."

"Does that happen often?"

"No, not really."

"How did you feel about it?"

"Well, mad, of course. And like he wasn't hearing me."

Bella looks down and makes a note in her book. Susan thinks about this. "Ironic," she mumbles to herself, just loud enough for Bella to hear her.

"Did your parents argue much, Susan?"

"Yes. My parents had a high-conflict marriage." Susan hated even thinking about her parents' marriage. Even remembering it was like walking through a minefield. Her mother wrote the original What Happens Here, Stays Here slogan, but in her case, the secrets didn't happen in Vegas, but in Home Sweet Home. Her mother swore her to secrecy, and before today, Susan had never broken that vow.

After waiting a few minutes for Susan to continue, Bella finally nudges her with a gentle question, "Can you explain?"

"Well, it's complicated. There were periods of time when my parents were the All American Couple. He was extremely handsome, my mom used to call him her Rock Hudson. And he was super charming. All my friends thought he was a movie star. To this day, if I run into any old friends who knew me when I was a kid, the first thing they'll say is 'We always thought your dad was a movie star.'" Susan sighs.

"My mom was pretty and slender and they were both very physically active and played games and sports and they were fun and popular. And then suddenly, ever so often, they weren't."

"What do you mean?"

"Ever so often, out of the blue, my dad wouldn't come home from work. Or he'd come home hours and hours late. Or sometimes he wouldn't come home for days."

"What would happen? How did that make you feel?" Bella leans in closer to Susan and Susan lowers her voice.

"It WAS awful. Mom would call everyone she knew, asking if they had seen him. She'd sit up and watch the late news, chain smoking, looking for car accidents. She'd call the hospitals, for God's sake. I'd be sent to bed, but I'd sit in my bedroom doorway, peeking out at the tv screen, trying to hear her phone conversations. I always felt like it was my job to see and hear everything."

"That's awful." Bella looks at Susan and they both get teary-eyed.

"It was awful." Susan sits and nods her head for a few minutes. Bella gives her space to gather her thoughts. She knows Susan will continue, there's no stopping now. "No one ever said it, but now I know that my dad was an alcoholic. A binge drinker. He'd be sober for months, on a health kick, weight-lifting, eating healthy, exercising and then all of a sudden, he just wouldn't come home. And then when he did appear, he'd be drunk. And the fighting would begin."

"Your mom would argue with him?"

"Oh yes, She was a hothead and she would, in one instant, go from being hysterically terrorized to being the hysterical terrorist."

"Did your mom drink, too?"

"No, not really."

"Did the arguments ever get violent?"

"Often they did."

"And did you witness this?"

"Yes." Susan simply says.

"And how would the arguments end?"

"Usually they went on for a couple of days and changed in tone. While my dad was drunk, he would be belligerent and argue back with my mom. Then the arguments would be very loud, stuff would get broken, Dad would punch his fist through a wall, my mom might get slapped, stuff like that. But eventually, they would fall asleep and he'd wake up the next morning with a hangover and an angry wife who would renew the argument. By that time, he'd be penitent and she'd still go ballistic."

"What do you mean by going ballistic?"

"Like this one time: My dad had been a factory laborer and with the help of his cousin, he sent out resumes and landed a job as a salesman. It was a really big deal to my dad. I remember him bragging about his resume. To him, it was as good as having a college degree." Susan almost smiles at the memory.

"So, anyway, my dad and mom went shopping and my dad bought a couple of suits. He was real proud of those suits. Those suits and his new hunting rifle made him feel like a successful man, I think. So one morning, after a big drunken fight, my mom got up and got dressed but my dad was still in bed, moaning and groaning about his hangover headache and he's wearing an icepack on his head and hugging a vomit bucket, and I was in the kitchen eating a bowl of cold cereal. Just a normal Saturday morning in the suburbs," Susan jokes to ease the tension.

Bella smiles and nods.

"The next thing I knew, my mom screamed at my dad and she grabbed his suits out of the closet, hangers and all, and threw them down in the narrow hallway that divided our house. Then she walked on them, wiping her shoes on the suits as she yelled at my dad. And then she returned to the bedroom and grabbed something else out of the closet and as I'm watching from the kitchen, she took his shotgun into the hall, grabbed it by the barrels and swung the shotgun into the doorframe, repeatedly, until the stock splintered." Susan pauses to catch her breath, feeling like she is running out of air.

"What happened then, Susan?" Bella hands Susan the tissue box, even though Susan is unaware she is crying.

"Well, Mom walked away and now the suits and the shotgun pieces litter the hall. I wanted to go back to my bedroom to hide out before anything else happened, so I walked around the suits and next to the shotgun, trying not to step on Dad's stuff. My mom saw this so she called me back into the front room and made me walk down the hall again, but this time, I am ordered to step on the suits and shotgun pieces. Dad's stuff was there most of the day and every time I had to go to the bathroom, or kitchen, I had to walk all over his stuff."

"Susan, I'm so sorry. How did the argument finally get resolved?"

"I don't know. I can't remember."

"Did this kind of thing happen often, Susan?"

"Maybe a couple of times a year." Susan blows her nose, wads the wet tissue into a tight ball, and reaches for a dry, fresh tissue.

"And was it always unexpected?" Bella makes another note.

"Yes. Although, as I got older, I learned to be able to sense when things were coming to a boiling point and I got pretty good at predicting the binges and outbursts."

"I forget, Susan, were you an only child?"

"No, I had a younger brother."

"What would he do when all this happened?"

"I usually kept him in my room and tried to make him feel safe."

"And do you and he ever talk about those times?"

"Not really. He seemed to think those kind of fights were funny. He actually laughed about them. And that day with the clothes in the hall? My bother walked up and down the hall at least 20 times that day, twisting and rubbing his dirty shoes all over everything. It was like a track event for him."

"That's an odd reaction."

"Yes," Susan agrees.

"Are you close to your brother?"

"He's dead," Susan answers quietly and Bella senses that's another story for another day.

"I'm sorry," Bella shakes her head.

"Thanks. We were estranged for many years. My parents' marriage took a toll on us. I asked Mom once why she stayed married to Dad all those years. She said they stayed together for the kids. Can you imagine?"

"My gosh. Did you thank her?" Bella snorts.

"No, I told her that when I was a kid, my nighttime prayers included me asking God to make my parents get divorced."

"Is that true?"

"Yes."

"I'm so sorry, Susan. Children should not be exposed to adult arguments. It changes who they are and usually results in children who grow up with trust issues."

"No kidding," Susan responds, then chuckles. "On the other hand, I have really good radar about people. I can spot an alcoholic a mile away."

"I bet you can," Bella nods and Susan bets that Bella has heard this observation often from adult children of alcoholics.

"Hey, do you think this family stuff has anything to do with my selective deafness?"

"I don't know. We'll find out." Bella glances at her watch and then asks, "Susan, have you been following the #MeToo Movement in the news?" Bella asks as if she's just making casual conversation, but Susan knows enough to know that there is no such thing as casual conversation in therapy. Every utterance is an oral inkblot test.

"Yes, as a feminist, I'm following it closely."

Bella nods. She waits and Susan waits, too. Then Bella asks, "And did you post #MeToo on your Facebook status?"

Susan smiles and can't help but admire Bella's interrogation skills. Just like that.

She asked The Big Question. Just. Like. That.

"Yes, I did." Susan answers. Just. Like. That.

"Do you want to tell me about your #MeToo experience?" Bella sets down her pen and crosses her legs.

"I've had a few, of course. Most women have. But I posted #MeToo because of my high school art teacher."

"What did he do?"

"He used to manipulate situations so that he could get behind me, like examining my art project, and then he'd rub himself up against my buttocks." Susan stops and looks up at the ceiling, recalling exactly what that art room looked like.

"How old were you, Susan?" Bella makes a note in her book.

"Seventeen. And still a virgin. Barely." Susan nods and laughs. "You know what I mean?"

"I do," Bella chuckles. "I was a 'barely virgin' myself at that time of my life. And Susan, where would this happen?"

"Usually right in the class room. That's how slick he was. And I couldn't say anything because I was afraid the other kids would notice and think I was a slut or something."

"It wasn't your fault. Not one bit."

"Oh, I know, I know precisely whose fault it was. But still, it made me feel trapped right there in front of everyone. Did they not see?" Susan shrugs her shoulders.

"I don't know what they saw, Susan. I'm sorry. You said 'usually'. Did this abuse occur in other locations, too?"

"Yes, I used to volunteer in the school library for one hour a day and he'd come down there and find me among the stacks of books and he'd find a way to get a hand behind me to rub my buttocks."

"How awful! What would you do?" Bella scowls at the thought of the adult teacher cornering a young girl like that.

"I'd walk away. I didn't want to turn around for fear he'd grab my front side, so I'd walk away as fast as I could. And know what?"

"What?" Bella asks, leaning closer and raising her eyebrows.

"As I walked away, he would chuckle!" Susan says, sounding angry.

"Wow!"

"Yes!"

"How did that make you feel?"

"Very. Very. Angry." Even after all these years, the memory makes Susan grimace.

"How long did it continue, Susan?" Bella asks, calmly.

"I don't know. Maybe about 3-6 months. I can't really remember. It started so casually, with him complimenting me and calling me a Cool Kid and asking me to model for his other art classes. He made me trust him and to tell you the honest truth, he made me get a little crush on him. He was cute, and older, and he thought I was cool." Susan nods at the memory.

"That's called Grooming. He was grooming you," Bella tells Susan.

"Damn. I never thought of it that way. He was grooming me!" Susan can hear the anger in her own voice and purposely lowers her voice, taking a deep breath.

"So, what happened, Susan. Can you tell me?"

"Yes, I can. I made a plan to confront him, and I did. I waited until the next time we were alone, which happened the very day after I thought of this plan. I was in the library and he came and asked the librarian for permission to borrow me in the art room. She agreed, of course. All the female teachers must have seen how cute he was. Anyway, he and I were walking down the hall and I positioned one of my arms behind me, waiting like a bear trap." Susan chuckles at the memory.

"And then? Did you catch a bear?" Bella asks, twinkling her eyes at Susan.

"Yes, I did! He reached over to grab my butt, and I grabbed his hand with my hand and I spun around and looked him straight in the face, still hanging onto his hand. I said, 'Do you see this?' And I held his hand up in front of his face. He said he saw it. Then I said, 'If this hand or any part of your body ever touches me again, I am going to tell my boyfriend who will come up to school and kick your ass. In front of everyone. And after that, I will tell my mom and she will make the biggest scene you have ever seen in your life. Right here at school. Do you understand?'" Susan looks at Bella and sees her smiling.

"And he said, 'I understand. And I'm sorry.' Then he walked away and I walked back to the library. It's a wonder I could walk, my legs were shaking so badly."

"Did he ever try to touch you again?" Bella asks.

"Nope. And guess what?"

"What, Susan?"

"I got an A in art!"

They both absorb that thought. Bella finally says, "You did a good job getting out of that situation. I'm sorry that happened to you. I'm also sorry that you didn't have any adults that you trusted enough to go to for help."

"Yeah, well………." Susan lets her sentence dangle.

"Susan, I can think of plenty of reasons you have to not want to hear men's voices," Bella says gently.

"I've thought of that, too," Susan agrees. "But all that was so long ago."

"Maybe you've got a little delayed PTSD?"

"Stirred up by all these #MeToo stories?"

"I've heard of stranger things," Bella says, standing up and smoothing her slacks.

"Whatever it is, do you think you can help me?" Susan asks, also standing now.

"I'm sure we can make you feel better. Shall we meet same time, next week?"

And that's how Susan figured out this whole selective deafness must be a big deal. Only big deals come to therapy every week.

Small deals come once every other week. Or even once a month. But the big deals, they have a standing weekly appointment. And it seems that not hearing what men say must be a big deal.

Especially to some people.

CHAPTER 6

S usan wakes up the following morning, feeling refreshed and confident that yesterday's therapy session may have done the trick. She thinks that the emotionally charged session served as a sort of re-booting of her system, and her hearing will be back to normal this morning.

Rolling over to face an empty bed, Susan remembers that today was Sam's early running date with Larry. Lately the two guys have been chumming up together a bit, going for short runs, having a quick game of tennis, or just watching a Saturday afternoon game. Whether this is an attempt to simply make a new friend, keep those Move More New Year's resolutions, or maybe some buddy support for a fellow husband with an impossible wife, Susan will never know. Nonetheless, she approves. Not that anyone has asks her.

Delaying the moment of truth, Susan pops into the bathroom for a few minutes. When she returns to the bedroom, she opens the miniblinds and looks out into the back yard, watching the squirrels digging up the daffodil bulbs. Susan taps on the windows, thinking she'll scare away the squirrels. They look at her, look at each other, and continue digging. Susan shakes her head and laughs. Yes, today is going to be a good day.

Susan climbs back into bed, fluffing her pillows into a perfect back rest and grabs the remote. She notices that her hand is trembling a little. She shakes her head in amazement.

"We're just turning on the television to check the weather," she says to no one.

"Here we go," she says as she points the remote at the cable box.

A few seconds later, *The Today Show* pops up on the screen. Hoda and Savannah are just finishing up a bit of Hollywood gossip, something about some Twitter argument between a late night host and the president of the United States. At one time, this would have been such shocking news, but today Susan hardly listens, this is such old news, and she's just waiting for any man to appear on screen and say something.

Savannah announces the weather and Susan holds her breath, waiting for Al.

But no, today's weather is presented by the smiling Dylan.

Susan sighs.

Should she change the channel, or keep waiting for a male guest, she wonders. She starts chewing on the inside of her lip, weighing her options.

And then suddenly, startling Susan half to death, the bedroom door flies open and Susan jumps. She starts to hop out of bed to grab the aluminum baseball bat when she sees a huge bouquet of yellow roses popping into the doorway and then heading her way.

She laughs.

Sam's face peeks out behind the roses. He's smiling that smile, the one that made her fall in love with him. And she smiles back.

He lifts his eyebrows at her.

She laughs. "Oh noooooo, did I forget another anniversary?"

He shakes his head No and looks her in the eyes and says something.

Probably he's saying something.

From the looks of it, it's something witty or cute or flirty.

Susan doesn't know.

She can't hear a word he's saying.

And without her saying a word, Sam knows this. He can read it in her eyes. His smile fades and his eyes grow misty. He sits down next to her on the bed, hands her the roses, kisses her on the forehead, and his lips move to form silent words.

"I love you, too," Susan says.

.

CHAPTER 7

Lauren: *Can U hear Dad yet?*

SUSAN: *Not yet. Soon, I hope.*

LAUREN: *How was your therapy?*

SUSAN: *Pretty good, I think.*

LAUREN: *What did she think about ur deafness?*

SUSAN: *She thinks that maybe it's some delayed PTSD.*

LAUREN: *Post traumatic stress disorder? That PTSD? From*
               what?

SUSAN: *From my childhood.*

LAUREN: *But that was AGES ago. lol*

SUSAN:

LAUREN: *LOL. So, she's saying that stuff happening 2 me*
             NOW can come back & bite me on the butt in 20 yrs?
             I better start saving 4 therapy. Student loans &
             therapy!!

SUSAN: *Apparently. What's happening to you now? Do you*
             want to tell me something?

SUSAN: *Should I call you? Is everything OK?*

LAUREN: *Besides my mom not hearing my dad? That's not*
             enough?

SUSAN: *I'm sorry, Lauren. This is not fun for any of us. I'm trying to make it better.*

LAUREN: *What r u trying?*

SUSAN: *Well, talking to Bella for one thing…….*

LAUREN: *What if that doesn't wrk? Poor Dad. I think his heart's broken.*

SUSAN: *Did he say that?*

LAUREN: *Not exactly, but I can tell. Do U still love him, Mom?*

SUSAN: *YES!!! Very much. Dad shouldn't be talking to you about this!*

LAUREN: *At least I can hear him!*

SUSAN: *Let's calm down. Let's not make this situation worse. It's bad enough, already*

LAUREN: *Did Dad tell U about his DM coming 2 town? He wants 2 take u & Dad 2 dinner. Dad thinks he's going 2 offer him a promotion r something……*

SUSAN: *Oh no! When is this supposed to happen?*

LAUREN: *Maybe in a week or 2. It's kinda a big deal. Dad
                doesn't wanna worry u about it, but he really needs
                U.*

SUSAN: *He should have talked to me about it.*

LAUREN: *Like U can hear him?*

SUSAN: *Lauren, that's not helpful. Maybe everything will be
                back to normal by then. I'm doing everything I can.
                I've smudged the house three times this week.*

LAUREN: *Are U meditating?*

SUSAN: *Of course. And I'm trying to be open to any lessons
                this is supposed to teach me. Maybe this is some
                karma thing.*

LAUREN: *From some past life? That's even longer ago thn ur
                childhood. Hahahahahahaha*

SUSAN: *Or maybe it's some unfinished business from a past
                life. Or maybe some lesson I didn't learn. Maybe this
                is an opportunity to learn some important life lesson.*

LAUREN: *So U think this is a punishment? U honestly believe that U owe some debt that has been passed down 2 this lifetime??*

SUSAN: *I know you don't really believe in karma, but a month ago, would you have believed it was possible for your mother to be deaf to male voices? There's more to life than what we can see & touch. You never know. Maybe, once upon a time, I did something that I need to atone for? Who's to say I didn't?*

LAUREN: *That's deep.*

SUSAN: *I wonder what the lesson could be?*

LAUREN: *Maybe ur supposed 2 buy ur daughter a car?*

SUSAN: *Haha. No, I don't think that's it.*

LAUREN: *Well, hurry up & fix this deafness thing as soon as U can.........*

SUSAN: *I am. I will. It will be a relief for things to get back to normal, won't it?*

LAUREN: *Yes. And there's someone I want U 2 meet……*

SUSAN: *Really?*

LAUREN: *Yes, I've been seeing someone. I want U 2 meet him.*

SUSAN: *Bring him home. I'll make a big dinner.*

LAUREN: *I can't.*

SUSAN: *Why not??*

LAUREN: *It's 2 embarrassing.*

SUSAN: *You're saying I'm too embarrassing?*

LAUREN: *Not U. Your condition.*

SUSAN: *I see. And what if my hearing never returns?*

LAUREN: *idk.*

SUSAN: *Life has to go on, Lauren.*

LAUREN: *I want things back 2 normal. I want U back 2 normal.*

SUSAN: *That's what we all want, baby.*

CHAPTER 8

Against her better judgement, Susan agrees to dinner with Sam and his DM. It happens on a Tuesday night at MVista, because, for some dumb reason, Sam believes this sham will be easier to swallow with a little soy sauce.

"You must think I'm a hell of an actress to be able to pull this off," Susan complains to Sam as he parks the car. "Remind me again: If I'm to agree, or respond with an affirmative answer to your manager, you'll smile at me. If my answer should be a negative response, you'll frown at me. And anything in between, I'll just try to read his lips? Is that still our plan?"

Sam flashes Susan a Thumbs Up.

"You know this will never work, right?" Susan asks, shaking her head.

Sam kisses Susan on her forehead as she exits the car, and pats her on her back. She just can't believe she has agreed to this farce.

Sam's DM is a handsome, 6 foot tall, ex-pro football player with a handshake that almost breaks several of Susan's knuckles. His thick black hair is cut short and his very being shines with confidence, almost to the point of cockiness. He towers over Sam and Susan suddenly understands why Sam found it so hard to say No to this tower of testosterone. He beams at Susan as they are introduced and leans over and whispers something to her.

"Nice to meet you, too," Susan responds. "I've heard so many nice things about you."

Both men smile, and Susan thinks she has passed the first test. The three of them are seated at a little table next to the bar. Sam and Mr Testosterone order drinks, Susan sticks with her Diet Coke, knowing she is going to need to be on her best game tonight.

The guys look at her and she smiles sweetly.

So far, so good.

The guys talk business, Susan guesses, because they wear serious faces. Susan does her best impression of an interested, supportive spouse. All of a sudden, Mr Testosterone says something to Sam and, in response, Sam smiles broadly and looks at Susan and continues to smile. She smiles back, doing her best impression of a happy, supportive spouse. Sam and Mr T shake hands, sealing some kind of deal. Susan looks over approvingly, nodding and smiling.

Then they turn to her and Mr T says something directly to Susan. Susan looks at Sam and can't read his signal. Is he smiling? Frowning? She can't tell. Winging it, she looks at Mr T and kind of shrugs her shoulders, trying for a neutral response.

"Omigosh, is that Larry over there?" she asks, pointing across the room at a man clearly not Larry. Sam looks around, then twinkles his eyes at Susan, catching on to her distraction trick.

Mr T raises his eyebrows at Susan, questioningly, probably confused by Susan's odd response.

Susan smiles at him and says something like, "Oh well," hoping that dinner will, please God, be over soon. For once in her life, Susan doesn't even want to see a dessert tray.

The guys laugh and the food arrives and Susan begins to feel hopeful that they might just pull this evening off. Sam looks happy, and really, that's all that matters to Susan.

Halfway through the salmon filets, Sam looks at his watch and stands. He says something to Susan and Mr T. The way he's holding up his hand, palm towards Susan, as he lays his napkin on the table, cues Susan that he's off for a quick bathroom stop. That signal, plus the fact that Susan already knows Sam's bladder is the size of a peapod.

As soon as Sam walks away, Susan realizes that she's alone with Mr T. He leans closer to Susan and she can almost smell his testosterone.

Oh boy, she thinks, I'm in trouble here. Susan doesn't need to hear words to recognize the look in his eyes. Any female over the age of 16 knows that look.

Smiling, Mr T reaches out and says something, touching Susan's hand with his fingertips.

Susan says, "Stop."

Mr Testosterone smiles with his too-white and too-straight teeth and traces his big index finger across the back of Susan's hand.

"Don't do that," Susan says, a little more loudly than she intended.

Mr T throws back his head and laughs. And then he lays his hand on Susan's thigh and whispers something to her.

Susan stands up with a quick jerk that upsets her chair.

The chair falls back into the table behind her and as Susan spins around to try to catch it, she loses her balance and starts falling over. Right into Mr T's waiting arms.

He laughs and says something.

Susan pulls away and says, "Don't touch me."

Mr T laughs harder. He says something and Susan sees that the waiter is also laughing and Sam is hurrying across the room. She can tell, even with no hearing, that he is furious.

"I'm sorry Sam," Susan says quietly.

He looks at her, not really understanding how so much has gone so wrong in the few minutes he's been absent.

"I'm leaving," Susan says to Mr T and to Sam. And to Sam's credit, he follows her out.

At the car, Sam helps Susan into her seat and signals her to wait one minute. "Okay," she responds, and Sam runs back into MVista.

A few minutes later, he returns to the car.

"It's not my fault, Sam. Let me tell you what happened," Susan begins, feeling awful about how things have turned out.

Sam nods at her, starts the car, and drives onto Gervais Street.

"Your DM made a pass at me, Sam."

Sam looks over at her and wears that same expression as when he sips unsweetened tea.

"I'm telling you the truth, Sam. He put his hand on my leg. On my thigh, for God's sake................" Susan hears her voice getting louder and her tone escalating, but Lordy, if your husband's boss making a pass at you doesn't deserve a harsher tone, what does?

Apparently, Sam disagrees.

He turns the car right onto Harden Street as Susan practically begs, "Sam, are you listening to me? It's wasn't my fault!"

And then Sam looks at her and starts talking, and Susan knows that if she could hear him, it would sound more like shouting than talking.

When his lips finally stop moving, she takes a deep breath, and calmly says, "I'm sorry I can't hear you, Sam. You know I can't hear a word you're saying."

Sam speeds up and they both ride in heavy silence. Halfway down Rosewood Drive, Sam pulls the car into the Publix parking lot and grabs his phone and texts,

He thought you were flirting with him.

"Oh Sam, darling. Don't you know, that's what these guys always say?" Susan hears the pleading in her voice and she halfway hates herself for sounding like that.

Sam texts his response:

> *I know, Susan. I know you weren't flirting.*
> *But maybe he didn't know that.*

"Sam! Listen to yourself!"

> *Listen to myself?*
> *Don't you mean READ myself??*

> *I'm out of patience!!*
> *This selective hearing nonsense has worn me out!!*
> *I need a TIME OUT.*

"I'm sorry, Sam. I'm worn out, too. Maybe we both need a time out."

> *I'm going to go visit my parents.*
> *You stay here and find your hearing.*

And that's the first night in all these years that Sam and Susan didn't share a bed.

Or a goodnight kiss.

CHAPTER 9

Susan A declares the next Susan Supper to be Mojito Night and all the Susans, and everyone else in Columbia, knows the best mojitos are served at Mr Friendly's New Southern Café. Sitting between a village of small shops and late-night bars and the university campus, perched practically right on top of the railroad tracks, Mr Friendly's, decorated with local artwork, feels like an oasis amid the loud college kids. A freshly mulled mojito, or two, accompanied by a Fried Green Tomato Stack, can cure most anything that's wrong. Or so the Susans hope.

"Here's to friendship," Susan A raises her glass and the other Susans clink her, smiling. Sipping their mojitos, three originals and one virgin, they share the same thought: Where would I be without these women?

"Well, damn it, how's everyone been this month?" Susan A looks around seeing that her friends' smiles have faded. "Look at us! Where did those smiles go?"

The Susans look at each other and see a lot of worries. No one speaks.

They sip their mojitos, enjoying the minty lime flavor. The waiter appears and they place their orders. As soon as the waiter turns to hand in their orders, Susan W looks at Susan S and asks, "So, evidently, your hearing hasn't returned to normal?"

Susan S shakes her head and frowns.

"Well, damn," mutters Susan A.

"What does your therapist think?" Susan W asks.

"She thinks we'll get to the bottom of this. Eventually. Meanwhile, she's trying to help me cope with the stress this is causing." Susan's eyes fill with tears and, like a yawn, the urge to cry spreads across the table. Not one dry eye. Susan M reaches out and lays her hand over Susan S's hand.

"Sam's mad at me. I'd say he isn't talking to me, but that would be ridiculous, considering the situation." Susan wipes the tears from her face, angrily.

"What happened?" Susan M urges.

"A couple of weeks ago, Sam's District Manager took us to dinner. I didn't want to go. I was sure it would end in disaster. I mean, he's a man and I knew I wouldn't hear one word he said. How could it be anything but a disaster? It sounds like a plot straight out of some corny made-for-tv movie, doesn't it?" Susan looks to her friends for support and they all nod in agreement.

"But nooooooo, Sam insisted. He said the company believes that no manager can do his/her job without the full support of their spouse and that I needed to be there for that dinner." Susan sighs. The other Susans wait. "So, ok, I went to dinner. And it was disastrous. Sam didn't tell him about my deafness and we tried to fake our way through dinner. Turns out the DM is a misogynist creep. He kept talking to me, and I couldn't hear what he was saying so I just kept smiling and then the minute Sam left us alone, he came on to me. It was a mess. I knocked over a chair. Everyone was looking at us. I made a scene. Sam was mortified. And somehow, I'm the one who came off looking like the Bad Guy. How did that happen?"

Susan struggles to not cry, so Susan M cries for her. "I'm sorry, I'm so sorry," she keeps saying, her empathy overflowing.

"Damn! Were you furious with Sam?" Susan A asks.

"Actually, Sam was mad at me. Madder than a hungry bumblebee in a glass jar."

"Holy Mother of God!" Susan W adds. "Then what happened?"

"So, of course, Sam and I get into a big argument on the way home. It started with me yelling at him and him nodding or shaking his head. Finally, he pulled over to the side of the road, right there in the Publix parking lot, and he took out his phone and start texted me."

"Holy shit," Susan A mutters.

"He told me that he thought this whole selective deafness thing was some kind of passive aggressive behavior on my part and I should knock it off!" Susan looks angrily at her friends. They respond by shaking their heads in disbelief and reaching out to touch her.

"Knock it off?" Susan W repeats, shocked that the Sam she knows actually believes Susan has any choice in this matter.

"He also said that he's going to visit his elderly parents for a week, or so, and I should use that time to quote, get my shit together, unquote." Susan empties her mojito glass and catches the waitress's eye for a refill. The other Susans raise their glasses for refills, too.

"So is he at his parents' house right now? In Phoenix?" asks Susan M.

"Yes!"

"I wonder if he's telling THEM the truth about your deafness," Susan W ponders.

"Who knows?"

"Well, dammit, I hate this! I hate this with my whole damn heart!" Susan A says, the anger in her voice almost visible.

Susan W sighs and shakes her head, making a mental note to discuss this with Larry when she gets home. She wonders what he thinks and if he could talk some sense into his new buddy. The way things have been between her and Larry lately, she's not so sure how open he is to listening to her.

Susan M continues to wipe tears from her eyes. When Susan S leans over to hug her, she apologizes, "I'm sorry. It's my stupid hormones."

"It's not just your hormones, it's the stupid men," Susan A corrects her. "Damn stupid men."

"Maybe the world would be a better place if we all grew deaf to men......" Susan M mumbles.

"Can you imagine a world where women can't hear men? What would that be like?" Susan W asks, honestly wondering.

"Heaven!" Susan A declares, than adds, "Seriously, Susan, tell us. What's it like not hearing the men?"

"Right now, I'd tell you it's pretty darn sweet," she laughs and the other Susans know she is laughing instead of crying. That's how she copes. "You'd be surprised how little you are told how to do every little thing when there are no men's voices. You'd be shocked."

"I wouldn't be too shocked," Susan W adds.

"And without men's voices, I'm beginning to feel less of a need to explain myself. Does that make sense?"

The Susans think about this, sipping their sweet drinks, each one thinking about how this applies in their own lives. One by one, they nod.

"And I feel less criticized. Well, until I read those texts last night."

"Maybe besides selective deafness, you also need to have damn selective reading skills, too! And sign me up, too, for a round of that, ya know?"

All the Susans laugh at the thought.

"Enough about me," declares Susan S. "I'm getting sick of talking about myself. Tell me about you. Who's on first?" she asks, laughing at her accidental joke.

"Well," Susan M starts, wiping away the last of her tears, "I told Dave that I'm pregnant. Actually, I had to, he got suspicious and confronted me, and I told him he's going to be a daddy."

"What did he say?" asks Susan S.

"He said, 'No, thanks.' Just like that. Like he was rejecting a second piece of banana pudding." She shakes her head and pats her tummy. "He said we have enough kids in the house already and we don't have room for another."

The food arrives and Susan M cuts her steak, calmly trimming off the bacon and slicing her steak into perfectly matched bite-sized pieces.

"Are you okay?" Susan W asks.

"Of course I am," Susan M answers with a bounce in her voice. "I don't care what he says. I mean, Dave is cool, he's a good cook and an imaginative and arduous lover but who am I kidding, you know those kids are my heart and I'll make as many as my uterus will produce."

"Well, damn, look at you go!" Susan A says, respectfully. "I love it. It's like you didn't even hear him. Ha!" Susan A pokes Susan S and they all laugh.

"And guess what else?" Susan M asks, shining with pride.

"What else?" Susan W asks.

"I was contacted by a popular wedding planner and I'm now going to be her official wedding baker. She'll send all her clients exclusively to me! So, with or without Dave, I'm still going to the wedding chapel."

All the Susans laugh. They enjoy a few moments of silence while they eat their dinners, forks flying everywhere as they taste from each other's plates.

"Ok, so Larry and I have been butting heads." Susan W starts and all the forks rest as the Susans turn and listen closely to Susan W.

"Oh, oh, what's up?" asks Susan A.

"Larry wants to move us to Chicago."

"NO! NO DAMN WAY!" Susan A starts to stand up in protest, but Susan S touches her gently on the arm which somehow triggers Susan A to sit quietly back down. She's sits quietly, but her hands tremble and her face is pale.

"That's exactly what I said," Susan W says directly to Susan A. Then, to everyone else, she adds, "He got a great job offer there and he really wants to take it. Of course, I could do my pottery business anywhere, but I don't want to move. I'm rooted here. I can't move someplace away from you!" Susan tightens her lips, trying not to cry. Susan M starts weeping again.

"Oh, Susan," Susan S whispers, sadly.

"He says I am being selfish. And immature. I have to confess, I did put my hands over my ears and refuse to listen to anything else he said."

"Damn!" Susan A says, "You made your own selective deafness!!"

"He's been sleeping on the couch the last three nights. We've been to counseling with the priest. I've been lighting candles and praying on it."

"Damn, I'm sorry. Is the whole world falling apart?" Susan A asks.

"What about you? We haven't heard from you. How are things with you?" Asks Susan W, happy to turn the spotlight away from herself.

"Not really so great," she says. "No men problems for me, hahaha."

The Susans laugh and Susan M asks the waitress for the dessert menu.

"So, what's going on?" Susan S prompts Susan A.

"I don't know. The greenhouse is finished, and it looks beautiful, but all my seedlings keep dying. It gets too cold in there and then I adjust the thermostat and it's too hot. Ha! Just like me. Is it me, or is it hot in here?"

They look at Susan A and see that she does look flush while they all seem comfortable enough.

"Is it your hormones? Are you starting menopause?"

"I don't think so. I'm not that damn old, am I?" Susan A asks, grabbing her water glass and gulping.

"Have you had your thyroid checked lately?"

"No, I guess it's time for a physical. Been a while. I'm just falling apart. Me and the greenhouse."

"Do you feel like you're falling apart?"

"Ha, I was just kidding. Or maybe not. I'm just feeling a little lost. Not like my old damn self. I don't know. Maybe I just need to get laid." Susan A laughs.

The other Susans nod, a little surprised.

"I'm kind of worried about my business. It's slow season, again, and the greenhouse ate up all my profits, and I guess I'm just a little worried about things."

"Oh, honey, what can we do to help?" asks Susan W

"Nothing. I'm fine, really." Susan A answers. "I just get overly anxious about money sometimes. Did I ever tell you I grew up kinda poor?"

"No, I didn't know that," Susan M answers.

"My dad was a groundskeeper for an estate across town. He loved his work, but it didn't pay much. I think I inherited my love for playing in the dirt from him. My mom worked at a grocery store as a cashier. Respectable, honest, hard-working people, but I tell ya, there was never any extra money. No trips to Disney for us. No brand name clothes. Lots of hand-me-downs. No new cars. We ate a lot of casseroles and peanut butter sandwiches. Thankfully, my dad grew vegetables in our backyard so we had plenty of fresh produce." Susan shrugs.

"Do you have siblings?" Susan M asks.

"Yes, an older brother and sister. I inherited all of his old shirts and jeans, and I wore her old dresses. To tell you the truth, I preferred his old clothes," Susan laughs, pointing down at her Nike shirt and UnderArmor jogging pants.

"Was it a hard childhood, Susan?" asks Susan S.

"No, it was generally good. It was just that I always felt a little inferior. Like, walking home from school, I'd pass those big houses in the fancy neighborhoods, and I always had a little envy. I know you're not supposed to covet thy neighbors stuff, but I coveted. I coveted their houses and their gardens and their fancy cars. Or at least I envied. And for some reason, even as a kid, I was keenly aware of class distinctions and I wanted the bigger house and the nicer things. But we didn't have that."

"I'm sorry. That sounds so sad. But you have lovely things now, Susan," Susan W points out. "We all have lovely things and so much to be thankful for, really."

"I know. And you're right. But that penny-pinching, coupon-collecting childhood has left me with a little money anxiety. So, you know, when the nursery business gets a little damn slow, I start to worry. Maybe I should be going to therapy, too."

"I think we all need therapy," Susan W declares.

"I think we all need dessert," Susan M suggests, showing the others the dessert menu. "Anything but cake. I've had enough cake this week."

CHAPTER 10

LAUREN: *U awake?*

SUSAN: *Yes, just sketching.*

LAUREN: *Got a minute?*

SUSAN: *For you? Always. Should I call you?*

LAUREN: *No, Maya is sleeping. Let's text.*

SUSAN: *OK. What's up?*

LAUREN: *Dad called me earlier. From NANAS!!!!!!! Y didn't*
              U tell me u r separated?

SUSAN: *Honey, it's just a temporary thing. A cooling off*
              period. Besides, Dad hadn't seen his folks in a while.

LAUREN: *My exams start this week. I really need 2 ace them 2*
              raise my grade.

SUSAN: *You should be studying right now.....*

LAUREN: *How can I when I'm worried about Dad?*

SUSAN: *About Dad??*

LAUREN: *About both of U, OK?*

SUSAN: *We're fine, Lauren. Everything will be okay. Just worry about your studies. Mom and Dad can take care of themselves.*

LAUREN: *Evidently not. Do U know that Dad cried on the phone?*

SUSAN: *Omigod. He should be talking to me, not you.*

LAUREN: *He says he can't talk 2 U.*

SUSAN: *That's just not true!*

LAUREN: *Dad and I think that U are deaf by choice. We think U could make it go away.*

SUSAN: *Do you now?*

LAUREN: *Yep. There's no other explanation.*

SUSAN: *This is completely out of my control. It's not my fault.*
             It's not anyone's fault. Sometimes, as they say, Shit
             Just Happens.

LAUREN: *Right.*

SUSAN: *Are you accusing me of faking this deafness?*

LAUREN: *Maybe not consciously.*

SUSAN: *Then what ARE you saying?*

LAUREN: *This isn't like the flu. No one else has it. You might*
             just b experiencing some hysteria, or something.

SUSAN: *Is that right?*

LAUREN: *All I know is this: Daughters of Divorced Parents*
             have trust issues their whole lives.

LAUREN: *DODP are less likely 2 marry & experience lower relationship commitments.*

LAUREN: *DODP have higher divorce rates. And, I'm sure that DODP cannot ace their final exams!!!!!*

SUSAN: *Lauren?*

LAUREN: *Yeah??*

SUSAN: *Go to sleep.*

LAUREN:

CHAPTER 11

"You started teaching this week, didn't you, Susan?"

Susan loves that Bella remembers. She also loves that she has a place where she can speak without filtering her thoughts.

"Yes, I did start. The first class was yesterday. I have 47 students in my class. My god, they're so young."

"Any chance they are all female?" Bella smiles.

"Nooooo," Susan laughs. "Almost a third are male. And no, I couldn't hear what any of them said."

"How did you handle that?" Bella asks, jotting in her pad.

"I just told them the truth. I began with 'A funny thing happened to me on the way to class' and then I explained that I couldn't hear the male students."

"How'd they take it?"

"Funny thing, the younger females in the class cheered. Can you imagine?" Susan laughs. "These younger women really make my day!"

"I know what you mean. They are spunky."

"Yes. And colorful. I never knew there were so many different hair colors. And guess what? Not one of the guys walked out. So, I guess we're set. I explained to them that they could text me or leave me messages on the class website. Fingers crossed, I think this selective deafness won't interfere too much with my teaching."

"That's great news. And has Sam returned home?"

Susan sighs. "He's still in Phoenix. He's working from home – his mom's home – and I'm not seeing a way to get him back here. He's really being heard-headed."

"Unless your hearing returns? That's his only condition?"

"Right." Susan frowns and shakes her head.

They sit in silence for a few minutes. Susan thinks Bella is waiting for her to add something else to the conversation, but she really doesn't know what else there is to say. She's running out of words. And patience.

Finally, Bella breaks the silence, "So, we've discussed your childhood. Your parents' conflicts. Your marital ups and downs.

Your relationship with Lauren…." Bella counts the items off on her fingers as she speaks, then adds, "I think it's time to quit looking back and start looking forward. What do you think, Susan?"

"Yes, let's look ahead."

"Have you given any thought on how you'll move forward if your complete hearing doesn't return?" Bella watches Susan closely as she asks her question.

"I haven't ever considered the thought that this condition could be permanent……"

"What if it is?"

"Then, I guess, it is. As Lauren would say, 'It is what it is.' I'll find a way to cope. Life will continue. And the good news will be, until we finally elect a female president, I'll never have to listen to the voice of another president." Susan smiles broadly at Bella.

Bella laughs and remembers, once again, why she likes Susan so much. Bella loves a survivor.

She schedules Susan's next appointment, two weeks away. Susan feels like she's just won a prize.

.

CHAPTER 12

After yesterday's therapy session and subsequent promotion to every other week therapy, Susan wakes up knowing that today is THE DAY. She's gonna hear Al Roker today and, rain or shine, his words are going to sound like sweet music to her ears.

Susan dances down to the kitchen for her daily Diet Coke and then back to bed, anxious to try the remote.

"Here we go, Al, talk to me, Baby!" she sings to the television, popping open her soda, taking a big drink, sitting it on the nightstand and grabbing the remote.

"C'mon Al, c'mon Al, give it to me, baby," she chants.

Susan switches on the television.

A commercial. Dammit. Susan listens to Ellen DeGeneres bragging about Spectrum Cable Company. Susan sips her Diet Coke and waits, whispering, "C'mon, Al, you can do it. Speak to me......"

The commercial ends and *The Today Show* begins. Savannah and Hoda are out on the plaza, greeting fans. Hoda kisses a sweet baby girl, and Savannah approaches a couple celebrating their 50th wedding anniversary. Savannah asks if they have dinner plans. The wife says she thinks it's a surprise. Her husband looks at her and smiles. And then, he says something that makes the wife cover her mouth with her hands.

Susan watches as the husband silently shows his wife a couple of tickets to some play and then he pulls a little blue box out from his jacket pocket. He hands it to his wife, saying something to her that Susan will never hear.

Hoda beams and announces, "Is that a box from Tiffany's?"

The wife pulls out a ring and places it on her finger. She looks at her husband with tears in her eyes. He says something to her, and in response, the wife replies, "Of course, I'll marry you again. I'd marry you a thousand times."

Susan switches off the tv.

"Yeah. Whatever," she says to no one in particular.

CHAPTER 13

S usan W looks at her watch and sees it's almost four o'clock. The Susans are meeting for supper at six, so she starts to clean her workspace. Susan lost all track of time today, a common phenomenon for creative people who have recently been visited by the muses. Susan believes that the muses visit more than one artist at a time with the same inspiration and that the first to carry it out to completion can call it her own, and Susan wants to call this design her own. Inspired by her dream of a vase composed entirely of the three Mystic Apes, Susan has enough self-awareness to recognize these Three Wise Apes represent her worries about her friend's partial deafness. This new vase design, if she ever gets it just so, will be christened *The Susan S*.

Wiping down the table, Susan is surprised to hear RING announce someone at the door. She hears the door open and shut, and before she has time to imagine a burglar or monster, Larry calls out, "It's me."

"Hey! What are you doing home this early?" Susan asks, worrying.

"I wanted to catch you before you went to supper. I was wondering if you can spare a couple of minutes to talk with me?" Larry asks.

"Of course," Susan answers, wiping her hands on her jeans and walking into the kitchen. "Wanna sit in here?" she asks, pouring herself a glass of water. "Want one?" she holds a glass out to Larry.

"Sure, thanks," he says. He drinks the entire glass of water as Susan watches, wondering where Larry wants to move now.

"I had lunch with Sam today," Larry says.

"Oh? I didn't know he was back in town."

"Yes, he just got in. I picked him up at the airport and we stopped for lunch on the way home."

"That's nice," she says, waiting for the other shoe to drop.

"We talked about Susan's deafness and his attitude. He's feeling very ashamed of the way he acted," Larry says, getting up and walking to the sink to set his glass in it. "We're both feeling like a couple of asses," he says quietly into the sink.

Larry turns and faces her. He lifts his face and speaks more clearly. "I'm sorry. I realize that I've been very selfish. All these years, you've followed me from place to place and never once complained. I want you to know I appreciate all your sacrifices. I recognize them and I appreciate them," Larry says, walking across the room to stand in front of Susan.

"Thanks. I don't know what to say……" Susan says, stunned. Larry has never apologized so beautifully before.

"Let me continue, if I may?" he pauses and waits for his wife's nod. "I think we can compromise here and both get what we want. Would you be willing to try?" Larry sits in the chair next to Susan and scoots it even closer to her.

"What do you mean, compromise? Move halfway to Chicago?" Susan raises her eyebrows, half in question and half in jest.

"I'd like to suggest that I still take the job in Chicago….."

Susan frowns.

"…….. but we don't move."

"Ahhhhh, how are you going to do that?" Susan asks.

"I'll commute." Larry gives Susan a minute to think about that and then explains, "I'll fly out ever Monday morning, or Sunday night, and return to you every Friday. The company has dorms up there and they offered me a room for weeknights, so it won't cost us anything. And they'll cover all the commuting costs. And maybe some weeks I can even work from home. At any rate, you can stay here, with your workshop and your beautiful pottery, and I'll go off to work and always return to you. Every week. Could we try that?"

Susan thinks about it. She has a thousand questions and a few fears about whether this can work, but she looks at Larry and realizes that even if the plan doesn't work, they still do.

She had almost forgotten that they were a team.

They could figure this out.

"And every Saturday night, we could have a date? Just like the Old Days," Susan W asks, twinkling her eyes at Larry.

"Yes!!" Larry says, loudly. "This could be the start of a new romantic era for us," he adds, putting his arms around her.

"Holy Mother of God!" Susan responds right before Larry places his lips on hers.

Meanwhile, halfway down the street, Sam sheepishly stands outside his own front door. He places his suitcase off to the side and arranges some cardboard sheets on the porch next to him. He straightens up, looks down for a minute, takes a deep breath, and then rings the doorbell.

After a wait that seems to go on forever, Susan opens the door and stares at him.

Sam puts out his hand and signals ONE with his index finger and then points at his watch.

"One minute?" Susan asks.

Sam nods.

Sam bends down and lifts up a handmade sign. He turns it over and holds it up for Susan to read.

I'm SORRY. It's my FAULT.

"Oh, Sam, what's your fault?" Susan wishes her voice didn't sound so impatient.

Sam nods and bends down and grabs his next cue card. He holds it for Susan to read.

I'm sorry. I want to be a better husband.

"Sam! I don't think it's anyone's fault. Come in, let's talk about this." Susan opens the door and tries to reach for Sam. He steps back and away and picks up another of his giant cue cards.

Can we go to counseling together??

"Of course, Sam, of course. And I know you believe that my deafness is some passive aggressive manifestation, but I swear on all my past lives that I don't bear any passive aggressive resentments towards you. I've always been able to share my anger with you, not repress it. And I know that there's always all those Battle of the Sexes jokes, but honestly, Sam, I don't feel any lingering resentment towards you. Or any man. I promise."

Susan steps out onto the porch with Sam.

Sam digs his phone out of his pocket and texts Susan.

Then what else can this deafness be?

"I don't know, Sam, I don't. And neither does Bella. But whatever it is, I'm sure it's not your fault."

And I'm sure it's not YOUR fault.

"Are you ready to come in now, Sam?" Susan opens the front door and tilts her head at Sam. She lets her eyes smile.

He grins and, in a flash, picks her up. He carries her over the threshold, and she laughs in delight. He laughs, too, and while she can't hear it with her ears, she hears it with her heart.

CHAPTER 14

Tonight's Susan Supper takes place at Motor Supply Company Bistro. It's a favorite Susan Supper choice, located in the historic part of downtown Columbia. The building, shared by an art gallery, was once a warehouse supplying motor parts for Georgia and South Carolina. Susan A loves the history of the restaurant and the specialty bar beverages, Susan M waited tables here for a short time between Baby #2 and Baby #3, Susan W loves eating so close to some of her favorite art pieces, and

Susan S shared her first dinner date with Sam in this same restaurant. It's always been a special place for the ladies and since, lately, they've all had their share of struggles, they unanimously decided this was a Motor Supply Company occasion.

As soon as they sit, in the recently enclosed back porch room overlooking the parking lot, Susan S announces, "I've got great news!"

"You can hear EVERY one?" Susan M asks, beaming with excitement.

"No. Not that. Sam is back home. We're reconciled. He's seen the light," Susan declares, sounding like an evangelist. "He's seen the light, ladies, and the light is practically blinding. It's like we're on our honeymoon again!"

"I'm so happy for you!" squeals Susan M.

"Good for Sam!" says Susan W.

"About damn time!" laughs Susan A.

"Yes, about damn time," Susan S joins the laughter. "Look, he knows he behaved badly and he's sorry. I don't think anyone can ask for more than that. Well, that and a fancy renewal of our wedding vows. Susan, will make us a delicious re-wedding cake?"

"You couldn't stop me from baking that cake!" Susan M says, all teary eyed. "Oh, here I go again. Nothing makes a pregnant woman cry more than happy news."

"So you're seriously going to renew your vows?" asks Susan A.

"Yes. And maybe by then I will be able to hear his!"

Everyone sits in silence, thinking about this and while everyone is happy for the reconciliation, Susan S suspects they don't hold much hope for the return of her hearing.

"What about Lauren? Is she behaving herself?" asks Susan W.

"Yes, her finals are over and she has accepted an summer internship at Hallmark cards. She'll be a temporary project manager for their website. Hopefully, that will lead to a full-time position. Of course, she will be away for the summer, but we're thinking that might be a good time for us all to spread our wings," Susan explains.

The three other Susans nod their heads and make no comments. Their salads arrive and no sooner are they placed on the table when Susan W announces, "More good news! Larry and I have found a compromise to our situation."

"Oh, oh, another compromise?" Susan A asks.

"Now hear me out. Larry is going to take the job in Chicago…"

"Such a surprise," mumbles Susan A and her sarcasm is thick.

"Let me finish, Susan. Larry is still accepting the job in Chicago, but we're not moving. He's going to commute. I'm staying here and he'll be home every weekend. I think that's fair, don't you?" Susan W turns and looks directly at Susan A.

"Yes, I'm sorry. Yes, it sounds damn fair. Sounds like a way for you both to get what you need."

"It sounds kind of lonely to me," Susan M adds.

"Not really, Susan. I'll be able to work on my new monkey vase design all I want now. No guilt for spending too much time in the studio. I think it sounds perfect."

"It sounds perfect to me, too, Susan," says Susan S, always in her friend's corner.

"It sounds pretty damn good to me, too. Sounds much better than a divorce," Susan A declares.

"Divorce is out of the question for me. But stubbornness is not," Susan W explains, sticking her fork into a crispy cucumber slice. "I guess we're just two stubborn old fools who want what we want. Me and those weiner dogs are staying put. And I think Larry is trying his best to hear me now. He's actually thinking about my needs."

The Susans think this over as their salad plates are cleared from the table.

"I have a little news, too," Susan A says in a quiet voice. None of the other Susans have ever heard Susan A speak so quietly before, and it makes them more than a little nervous.

"Well, tell us!" Susan M says, looking like she's about to pop. And considering she's in the beginning of her third trimester, no one wants to see Susan M pop. Not yet.

"I kissed a girl," Susan A announces.

"What?" Three Susans ask, all together.

"I kissed a girl," Susan A giggles. The other Susans stare at her, never having heard a giggle erupt from Susan before. They stare, Susan giggles again, and the Susans all break into grins.

"Did you now?" Susan S asks. "Spill the details, girl!"

No one is eating now. No one is even holding their forks, their breath, yes, but not their forks.

Susan, beaming with pride, continues, "Actually, a girl kissed me. Well, the first time, she kissed me. The second time, I kissed her."

And suddenly, the joy on Susan's face spreads across the table and all four Susans wear the same expression that can best be described as the perfect blend of delight and curiosity. They wait for Susan to continue, and of course, she does, "She's a botanist. Let me show you her Facebook page."

Her fingers shaking, Susan A pulls her iPhone from her pocket and opens her Facebook app. It opens right up to the profile photo of a cute blonde standing knee deep in swampy water filled with lily pads. "What do you think?" asks Susan A.

"I think she's adorable!" exclaims Susan M. "Oh, this is so romantic," Susan says, wiping her eyes.

"Damn right," says Susan A. "Damn right!" Susan looks around the table and doesn't see a trace of disapproval, so she continues, "We're going on a date this weekend. What do you think?"

"I think 'Why not?'" Susan W answers while the other two Susans nod in agreement.

"That's what I thought. I thought, Hey, I'm through with men, I really am, but does that mean I'm through with relationships? Maybe it doesn't."

"Maybe it doesn't," Susan W agrees." And does she mind that you're straight?"

"Am I? Am I straight? Am I gay? Am I a mix of the two? Who knows? Why do we need labels? I just don't know. And, maybe we'll just be friends. Or maybe it will turn into more. Who knows? Life is damn funny, ya know? But, I've decided that I'm open to this opportunity, and my friends, my heart beats faster every damn time I hear her voice."

"Go for it," Susan M says, before anyone else can say a word.

"I agree," Susan W says.

"It's unanimous," Susan S chimes in.

By now, their food is cold and no one seems to care, everyone just feels so contented. Susan M smiles at her friends and announces, "It's an evening for announcements, it seems, and here's mine," Susan says, rubbing her belly, "I'm having a baby girl."

"Isn't that perfect! You'll have two boys and two girls!!!" Susan A declares.

"Oh, I can't wait to start shopping for pink stuff. I love the pink stuff!" says Susan W.

"Congratulations, Susan. A sister for Patrick, Oprah, and Barry. Have you picked out a name?" Asks Susan S.

Susan M throws her head back and laughs, "You know I have."

The other Susans laugh and can't wait to hear this conception story. Susan M always tells the best conception stories, but the Susans are convinced the Oprah story in the Nickelodeon will be a hard to beat.

"I'm naming her Luna," she looks around the table expectantly. "Get it?"

"Like the moon?" asks Susan W, and Susan M nods.

"Did you conceive her under a full moon?" asks Susan A.

"Nope."

"During a blue moon?" asks Susan S.

"Nope," Susan M laughs. "Give up?"

The three non-pregnant Susans give it a minute's thought and then all practically shout, "Tell us!"

"Remember the solar eclipse?" Susan M grins at them. "Remember how the moon hid the sun and made the world dark?" Susan M pauses for dramatic effect. "Did you not feel the magic when that happened?"

The Susans nod, remembering that eerie moment.

"In that moment, when the world was dark, and the birds chirped and the stars came out, I felt like my heart would burst with love. I looked over at Dave and saw his eyes mirror what I felt in my heart. Thank goodness the kids were at their daddies' houses because the minute I saw that look on his face, I dragged his sweet ass into the house and we made Luna. My Luna," Susan M smiles at the memory. "I'll think of that special moment every time I look into my Luna's eyes, I just know I will." Susan M beams, eyes full of tears.

"That's a great story," Susan S declares and the other Susans smile and nod their heads in agreement.

"Things going better with Dave?" asks Susan A.

"Things are fine. Just fine," says Susan M, and she picks up her fork and starts eating.

The Susans finish their dinners with much laughing and talk about local politics, their favorite new books, and Susan's new monkey vase design. They order a crème Brulee and four spoons and sit in happy contentment, looking out over the parking lot.

"Look at this kid! What in the hell is he doing?" Susan A asks, peering out into the parking lot.

And the Susans look in time to see a boy marching slowly across the parking lot holding a big bunch of floating pink balloons.

"What is that?"

"Is that some kind of delivery service?"

"Or a promotion for a new movie?"

And, by now, everyone in the dining room turns to watch the boy. They all sit, squinting into the sunny parking lot to see what's happening.

Everyone except Susan M.

She's standing.

And then, as the patrons watch the balloon boy marching across the parking lot, they see that he is followed by a pretty young girl, carrying a big bouquet of long-stemmed pink roses. The roses must be heavy, or awkward to carry, because the little girl is hanging onto them by the stems and the rose blossoms are dragging across the parking lot, leaving a trail of pink petals.

"What the hell?" Susan A says, loudly.

"Some publicity stunt?" Susan W asks, quietly.

"No. It's MY kids," Susan M practically whispers, as she stands, hands over her heart. The other Susans don't know whether to watch their friend, or the spectacle happening outside, which, by the way, is gathering a crowd of observers, most of them holding up their cell phones.

And then, another boy joins the parade, and he's carrying a tray of something that looks like a couple of cupcakes lit with birthday candles.

"Is that little Barry?" Susan A whispers to Susan M who just nods and holds her heart while tears rolls down her cheeks, but she doesn't care, she's not looking away from those kids, who by now, have turned and are headed toward Motor Supply's door.

Everyone in the room turns and watches the doorway, waiting to see what's going to happen next. There's not a heart in the room that isn't beating a little faster than normal. All the women in the room are smiling, and the men are shaking their heads and trying not to look too sentimental. Everyone embraces this moment.

Especially the Susans.

And especially one Susan who now steadies herself by holding onto the back of her chair.

Into the room marches Patrick, pink balloons and all. His back is straight; he's not the least uncertain of his mission. He looks around, spots his mother, and marches directly to her, handing her the balloons, and giving her a sweet little bow. He turns, as if he's practiced this a thousand times, and he waits for his sister, who marches into the room carrying her pink rose stems which, by now, are practically flowerless. Oprah hands the flowers to her mom, curtsies, and stands next to Patrick, both watching the door.

After a three second delay, in marches little Barry and the cupcakes. He hands them to his mommy and kisses her on the cheek before he runs over to join his siblings.

The room is so quiet that no one seems to be even breathing.

And then suddenly, the most handsome man in a tuxedo struts into the room. As he passes the three kids, he pats each one on the top of their head and when he does, the kids grin and stand up super-straight.

This tall, dark, handsome guy turns towards Susan M and kneels in front of her.

"Will you PLEASE be my wife and make my life complete?" he asks, loud enough for even the kitchen staff to hear. It's as if he wants the whole world to hear. "Will you PRETTY PLEASE marry me and make me the luckiest man in the world? I promise to love you and our kids forever, however many we have," he twinkles his eyes at Susan M and right there, at that moment, there's not a woman in that room who isn't in love with Dave.

CHAPTER 15

S usan S is absolutely sure that when the sun rises, her hearing will be restored. It will just be the perfect ending to a perfect 24 hours. She falls asleep, snuggled up against Sam, and the only thing she's wearing is a silly-ass grin.

At 7:00 am, she receives a text and like all good mothers, she jumps out of bed and grabs her phone. She sees the message is from Lauren.

LAUREN: *OMG, Mom!!!!! Sorry 2 wake U but U gotta see this.*

LAUREN: *https://tweeter.com/chrissyteigen/status/9997808659*

LAUREN: *Did U read it? John Legend's wife has ur case of*
            Selective Deafness!!!!!!

SUSAN: *WHAT??? This is the weirdest thing!! What does it mean?*

LAUREN: *It means U R not crazy!!!!*

SUSAN: *HOLY COW!*

LAUREN: *MOM! Read the Comments. There are other women who can't hear men. OMG! OMG!*

SUSAN: *You do that and I'll turn on the tv and see what they're saying………..*

Susan gets up and tiptoes into the family room, where she switches on the tv. She sits in the dark with the volume low and she sees that Savannah and Hoda are sitting at a news desk, talking to the camera. As the tv screen pops into focus Susan hears Savannah announce, "The CDC in Atlanta has just confirmed almost twenty unrelated cases of mysterious auditory phenomena. This condition only occurs in women."

Hoda reads, "Only in women. So now, besides cramps and bloating, women are having hearing problems?" Hoda plays to the camera, looking for a laugh.

"And not just any normal auditory issue, Hoda," Savannah continues. "It's a Selective Hearing issue. Apparently, the women pass all the standardized hearing tests. They can hear perfectly, as long as they aren't listening to a man's voice."

"What? Are you saying they can't hear male voices?"

"That's right, Hoda. The women are deaf to men's voices. They cannot hear a man – any man – speak." Savannah is wearing a solemn expression, but as Susan leans forward and looks more closely, she thinks she sees Savannah's eyes smile.

"Well, it's about time!" declares Hoda, as she nods her head.

And Susan can't help herself, she nods along with Hoda.

THE END

Acknowledgements

It takes a lot of hands and eyes and hearts to write a book and I'm lucky enough to be surrounded by generous and skilled friends & family. I'd like to especially thank Mary T Smith who guided me in the right direction and helped me tighten the beginning. Thank you to Donna George who read with her heart and encouraged me every inch of the way. I'm grateful for Sheryl P Maffett who knows how to edit with a gentle hand and a true voice. To Jan Perez and Suzanne Sloan, my early readers, I appreciate your feedback. Thank to Keith for all the read-aloud hours and for listening to all my ideas. And special thanks go to Adam Smith, who reminded me to return to the keyboard.